"I've come to ta... doctor."

Slade clenched his jaw. "It's only a... drive, but I don't know how long it takes you to do…whatever it is that women need to do to be ready to go out."

Laney laughed. He raised a brow, but she only shook her head.

What had he said that was so funny?

Women. He'd never understand them, and frankly, he didn't even want to try. Especially this one.

If it weren't for Brody's baby, he'd be out of there so fast Laney's head would spin. It was asking a lot just for him to be in the same room with her, but for Brody's kid, Slade would grit his teeth and try to get through it.

"I'm a wash-and-wear kind of girl," she informed him, tossing her hair over her shoulder with an animated flip of her hand, which to Slade felt like a major brush-off. "I'll be ready in five. And I'm going to ignore the fact that you just tried to order me around again."

His gaze widened on her and he hoped he wasn't gaping.

"But don't do it again."

Deb Kastner is an award-winning author who lives and writes in beautiful Colorado. Since her daughters have grown into adulthood and her nest is almost empty, she is excited to be able to discover new adventures, challenges and blessings, the biggest of which is her sweet grandchildren. She enjoys reading, watching movies, listening to music, singing in the church choir, and attending concerts and musicals.

Books by Deb Kastner

Love Inspired

Email Order Brides Series

Phoebe's Groom
The Doctor's Secret Son
The Nanny's Twin Blessings
Meeting Mr. Right

Serendipity Sweethearts Series

The Soldier's Sweetheart
Her Valentine Sheriff
Redeeming the Rancher

Cowboy Country Series

Yuletide Baby
The Cowboy's Forever Family

Visit the Author Profile page at Harlequin.com for more titles

The Cowboy's Forever Family

Deb Kastner

If you purchased this book without a cover you should be aware that this book is stolen property. It was reported as "unsold and destroyed" to the publisher, and neither the author nor the publisher has received any payment for this "stripped book."

Recycling programs for this product may not exist in your area.

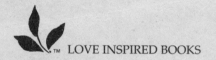

LOVE INSPIRED BOOKS

ISBN-13: 978-0-373-87944-1

The Cowboy's Forever Family

Copyright © 2015 by Debra Kastner

All rights reserved. Except for use in any review, the reproduction or utilization of this work in whole or in part in any form by any electronic, mechanical or other means, now known or hereinafter invented, including xerography, photocopying and recording, or in any information storage or retrieval system, is forbidden without the written permission of the editorial office, Love Inspired Books, 233 Broadway, New York, NY 10279 U.S.A.

This is a work of fiction. Names, characters, places and incidents are either the product of the author's imagination or are used fictitiously, and any resemblance to actual persons, living or dead, business establishments, events or locales is entirely coincidental.

This edition published by arrangement with Love Inspired Books.

® and TM are trademarks of Love Inspired Books, used under license. Trademarks indicated with ® are registered in the United States Patent and Trademark Office, the Canadian Intellectual Property Office and in other countries.

www.Harlequin.com

Printed in U.S.A.

And God will wipe away every tear from their eyes;
There shall be no more death, nor sorrow, nor crying;
And there shall be no more pain,
For the former things have passed away.
—*Revelation* 21:4

To the Texas Tenors: John Hagen,
Marcus Collins and JC Fisher.
I'm incredibly grateful for your beautiful music.
My Texas Tenors playlist has accompanied me
through many tight deadlines,
and this book is no exception. Thank you!

Chapter One

"I miss you, buddy."

Slade McKenna's throat burned and he swallowed hard. He shook his head and grunted at his own foolishness. He wasn't in the habit of talking to those who'd passed on. Thankfully, no one was here to witness the rarity.

Stirrup-high Texas grass brushed across his boots as he rode the fence line in search of bent posts or breaks in the barbed wire where the Becketts' cattle might get free. Mending fences kept his mind off the bad stuff.

Mostly.

He wasn't the kind of guy who expressed emotion, verbal or otherwise, but right now his feelings were digging as deeply into his side as spurs, no matter how hard he bucked and resisted to throw his grief.

His best friend Brody Beckett was gone. Forever. *Dead.*

He could hardly bear to *think* the word, much less say it aloud, especially when Brody's absence was such a stark, bitter reality. Checking the fences on his parents' ranch property had been Brody's chore since he was old enough to sit straight on a horse, and as his best friend, Slade had often accompanied him in his rounds. When they were both little tykes, Slade and Brody had spent many hours out here on the range together, where the lowing of cattle, the gentle Texas wind and the creak of saddle leather were the only sounds to break the sweet silence.

That, and the howling and hollering of a couple of ornery young boys who'd rather have been wrestling than wrangling.

Riding and roughhousing with Brody. Those were some of the best memories Slade had. And all of Brody he had left to take with him now.

Memories.

Slade pulled his mount up, clenched his jaw and concentrated on pushing his thoughts—and the pain—away.

His black quarter horse mare Nocturne shifted sideways and pricked her ears forward. Slade was suddenly alert and completely attuned to both his mount and his surroundings. His eyes narrowed as he scanned the area for the prospect of danger, thankful for the shadow of the brim of his black Stetson against the glaring sun.

He knew his horse as well as he knew his own thoughts. Nock's muscles twitched underneath him. He tightened the reins and squeezed his knees to encourage his horse to remain steady. The hair on his arms stood on edge from the crackle of tension in the air and he strained to listen to the sound of movement within the silence. He didn't know what was wrong, but he had no doubt there was something out there on the Texas prairie. Nocturne wasn't easily spooked.

A snake? A cougar?

But it wasn't the sound of rattling Slade's keen ears picked up on.

Instead, he heard sniffling, coming from just over a rolling mound of earth only a few feet away.

Adjusting the brim of his hat low over his brow, Slade dismounted, leaving Nocturne to graze. He approached the direction of the unlikely sounds cautiously, unsure of what he'd find—or rather, who he was about to encounter. Frankly, he'd rather face a whole pack of hungry coyotes than one weeping female.

If he had to guess, he expected her to be a teenager, one of the local girls who'd just had her heart broken and was hiding out trying to sort her emotions. Bit far out of town for a kid, but she'd probably parked near the fence and decided to walk for a while. Not the smartest idea. A girl could be easily lost. But she probably wasn't thinking straight.

Adolescent angst. Just what he didn't want to have to deal with today.

Slade's first thought was that he shouldn't interfere with whatever drama was going on in the Becketts' backyard. He hadn't yet made his presence known. He could turn around, mount up and ride away and the Mysterious Crying Female would be no wiser for him having been there at all.

He had no business here. For starters, he wasn't any kind of expert in female drama, teenage or otherwise. If the girl was hiding out here fairly far out on the range to have a good cry, she probably didn't want to be found or interrupted, especially by a guy like him.

On the other hand, he couldn't very well walk away if the poor kid needed his assistance. It wasn't in him to leave when he might be needed. He was a cop, for one thing. Helping people was his day job. He figured he ought to at least check her out and make sure she wasn't hurt, even if it did make him feel every kind of awkward. And it was what God would expect him to do, right? Help his fellow man—er, woman?

But consoling a teenager? *So* far out of his comfort zone. This newfound faith of his was going to be a whole lot harder than he'd imagined when he'd first bowed his head at the cowboy church and acknowledged the Almighty.

The ranch was private property, but Brody's parents wouldn't be too bothered by a girl seeking out somewhere to be alone and find some solace. In fact, they'd be urging him to help her out, since he was the one to find her.

He shoved out a breath, resolving to be nice to the kid. Patient, if he could manage it. He wasn't known for that particular virtue, or many others, for that matter. But he would try.

Yanking his Stetson from his head, he topped the grassy mound, his shadow engulfing the female huddled on the other side. "Excuse me, miss, but I was riding by and I couldn't help but overhear—"

His sentence slammed to an abrupt stop at the same moment his gaze met a pair of fiery brown eyes showering sparks at him.

"You." His voice formed around the word like an accusation because that's exactly what it was. "What are you doing on Brody's property?"

Laney Beckett, Brody's estranged wife and now his widow, scrambled to her feet, all five feet and nine inches of her. She raised her chin and brushed the moisture from her cheeks with the sleeve of her lavender-colored shirt. She might be on the taller side for a woman, but Slade stood at six-two when he was slouching and he towered over her. He squared his shoulders and used his superior height to his advantage.

"I could ask you the same thing, Slade McKenna," she countered, apparently unfazed by his attempt to intimidate her.

Fury rushed through him, heat rising from the heels of his boots until it burned in his ears. It was all he could do to rein in his temper. He curled the brim of his Stetson until his knuckles were white.

She crossed her arms in a paradoxically defiant and defensive gesture. It was only then that his gaze shifted away from her eyes—and straight to her burgeoning middle.

Slade's breath slammed from his lungs as if he'd been sucker punched. He scowled in disbelief.

The woman was pregnant. Had he lived, Brody would have been a *father*.

Slade clenched his jaw, afraid he was gaping, or that he'd say something he'd later regret. Emotion surged through him. He was angry, shocked, grief-stricken and indignant on Brody's behalf, all at once, and he didn't know what to do with any of the feelings consuming him.

Brody couldn't have known about it. Slade was certain of that fact. Laney must have been pregnant at the funeral, but Slade certainly hadn't been the wiser for it. She hadn't *looked* pregnant. But she must have known she was carrying Brody's baby, even back then. How could she take off without even sharing that information with anyone? It made him sick just to think about it.

He spun away from her and stalked several yards,

scrubbing a hand through his thick black hair and forcing raspy breaths into his lungs.

"Why are you here *now*?" he growled. "Especially in that—" he waved a hand in the general direction of her protruding midsection "—condition? It certainly didn't take you long to hightail it out of Serendipity after the funeral. With Brody's baby, no less."

"I don't answer to you," she responded, her tone deceptively quiet and even. It wasn't hard for him to hear the barely concealed disdain for him in her voice.

He couldn't care less what Laney thought of him. His only concern was for Brody's honor and memory, for which Laney obviously cared so little. And what about Brody's folks? Did Grant and Carol know they had a future grandchild?

Brody's baby. How was this even possible? Laney and Brody had been separated. And now she was pregnant? How could he have missed that fact when Laney was here for the funeral? A looming sense of guilt and responsibility clouded Slade's thoughts.

Brody's baby.

"You owe me some answers," he pressed, turning to face her full-on. One way or another, she was going to tell him everything.

She sputtered and gasped. Her irises flared, darkening the chocolate brown of her eyes. "You are the most arrogant, self-absorbed man I have ever met in my life. This isn't about you, and I'm certainly under no obligation to answer to you. What would possibly make you think I'd tell you anything, especially after the way you've treated me today with all your blustering and bullying?"

Slade flinched. He was many things, but he wasn't

a bully. Maybe he *was* trying to intimidate her a little bit, but for good reason. He was after the truth. And Laney *did* owe him that much, even if she didn't acknowledge it right now. He had an obligation toward that baby. But maybe he was approaching her wrong, although he didn't have the slightest idea how to fix that problem. He took a mental step backward, regrouping his forces against the stubborn woman.

"Brody was my best friend." Nothing like stating the obvious, but he had to say *something* to fill the awkward void left by her question.

"He was my husband," she launched back, spitting the words. "Not that you would have any idea about the kind of commitment a man and woman make to each other."

He hissed through his teeth. He had less use for love than he did for Laney. Just look at what it had done to Brody. He glared at her belly rather than meeting her gaze. One way or another, he was going to pull the truth from her.

"I don't understand. You didn't even look pregnant at the funeral, and now you just show up in Serendipity out of nowhere." A statement of fact, even if it resembled an indictment. "What's your angle, Laney? Why are you really here?"

What was her angle? What was her *angle*?

How dare he?

Laney pulled in a deep breath through her nose in an unsuccessful attempt to force herself into a state of calm she didn't feel—not so much for her sake but for the baby's. If it wasn't for the little one growing inside her, she might very well have launched herself at

Slade and really given him the what-for he clearly deserved. She had the notion he'd never been walloped by a woman before, and it was high time he was taken down a notch or two.

Or ten.

Despite her best efforts, her heartbeat roared in her ears and her pulse skyrocketed. If real smoke could blow from her ears she'd be steaming like a kettle right now.

"I wasn't yet showing at the funeral, but I knew I was carrying Brody's baby."

His piercing blue eyes narrowed on her and he stepped forward, looming over her and puffing out his chest like a rooster. As if *that* would intimidate her. She was exactly right in saying he was nothing but a schoolyard bully.

"How did this happen?" His voice was low and icy.

"Excuse me?" Both of her eyebrows arched, disappearing under her hairline. If Slade didn't know the facts of life she certainly wasn't going to be the one to explain them to him. The very idea was laughable.

"You and Brody were having a baby together, when I know for a fact you two were separated well before his—" He paused and his voice deepened and turned gruff "—accident happened."

"Obviously, we spent some time together trying to work things out," she retorted, clipping her words. "He was my husband," she reminded him again.

"That doesn't necessarily mean anything."

Wow. He might as well have slapped her. She could give and take as well as the next woman, but it wasn't only her character he was maligning. It was Brody's.

And Slade was casting a shadow over their beloved baby, as if the unborn Beckett was some kind of mistake.

"You can't imagine how I felt when I discovered I was pregnant," she informed him coldly. "I was so happy. So angry. And horribly, horribly saddened by it all. I'm responsible for raising Brody's baby all on my own. He or she is all I have left of my husband."

He shrugged. "But you sure didn't take any time after his death to grieve for him, did you? You ran away to—wherever—instead of sticking around."

"Take that back." She shoved at his chest and he immediately raised his arms in surrender.

"I'm only saying how it looked to me."

"Then maybe you need to get glasses. Not to mention giving me—and Brody—a little more credit."

He jerked his chin. She wasn't sure whether he was agreeing with her or merely acknowledging what she'd said.

"I had my reasons for leaving town after the funeral. And Brody and I *were* trying to work it out," she reiterated, in case there was any doubt whatsoever in the big oaf's mind. "Brody is the only man I've ever loved. But it didn't help that you put ideas in his head, did it? Led him away from his family obligations without a care for how it affected me. Don't you have a conscience?"

He had the good grace to flinch, but the way he was eyeing her rounded middle, as if weighing her words for truth, made her want to cover her belly with her arms to protect the child within.

"Why were you crying?"

His question caught her off guard, not only the words themselves, but the muted tone in which they were asked. Surely he hadn't picked now to decide to control that wicked tongue of his. He'd already done too much damage to go back now.

"I—" She started to deny she'd been crying at all, but that would have been a lie. She *had* been crying. He'd caught her with tears pouring down her cheeks. She couldn't very well deny it now. "Sometimes my emotions catch up with me. I try to keep them in check, but every so often, something reminds me of Brody and it's just too much of a burden for me to bear."

"Yeah," he agreed, sifting his finger through his thick black hair. "I know what you mean."

He probably did, at least to some degree. For all his faults, Slade had been Brody's best friend and had known him from childhood. He had to be hurting, too, she supposed, in his own ill-mannered way. Maybe that was part of the reason he was acting like such a Neanderthal. Not that that was any excuse for the way he'd treated her when Brody was still alive...

"Where are you parked?" he asked gruffly.

"Back at Brody's folks' house." She glanced around her but saw only grassland in every direction. It all looked the same to her. She hadn't realized she'd wandered so far from the homestead. Not only could she not see the house from here—she didn't even know from which direction she'd come.

She was lost.

Not that she'd admit that particular fact to Slade.

"You walked all the way from their *house* in your condition?" He looked her up and down, disbelief in his gaze. "Do you know how many miles that is? What were you thinking? You could have hurt yourself or the baby."

"I'm pregnant, not ill. It's perfectly acceptable for me to walk. If anything, it's a good thing for me to get all this fresh air and exercise." Maybe she shouldn't have wandered *quite* so far off onto the range, but she hadn't been thinking.

Or maybe she'd been thinking too much.

He didn't look the least bit convinced she wasn't taking unnecessary risks. Well, too bad for him.

"You'll never make it back to the house before dark on foot." How did the man make every single statement out of his mouth sound like an accusation? Then again, she had to concede that he did have a point.

Heat flushed her cheeks. She'd left midafternoon. It had never occurred to her that she might be caught with the sun setting on her. She might be fine now, but she'd be completely helpless in the dark. Of course, she hadn't planned to walk quite this far.

Or to get lost.

"You don't even know where you are, do you?"

As much as she'd hated the accusatory tone he'd used on her earlier, at least she'd known how to respond to it. What she heard now was sympathy, with a note of kindness. Where had that come from?

She didn't answer, shifting her gaze to somewhere over his left shoulder.

"You don't."

He didn't have to sound so satisfied.

"It's settled, then. You're coming with me."

She ignored his dictatorial attitude. She would argue all night about his high-handedness if it was just her at risk in the dark with no clear route home, but she had the baby to consider, and pride only took a pregnant woman so far. "All right, I guess. You've got your truck parked somewhere nearby?"

He laughed, a deep, rich rumble from low in his chest. "Something like that."

"Why do I feel like I should be worried?"

He chuckled again and took her hand to steady her as they walked over the uneven soil. She allowed it, but only because the increase in her waistline made her steps ungainly. Laney might not be a country girl, but she was a native Texan and she knew the wild terrain was filled with treacherous bumps and hollows along the way.

As they crested the hill she saw why Slade was hedging. His mode of transportation was a horse, not a truck, contentedly grazing on the grassy knoll.

So much for a comfortable ride back to the house. Did he really expect her to get up on that thing, as pregnant as she was?

Slade whistled and the black mare lifted her head. A second whistle and she trotted to his side. It was the most unusual thing she'd ever seen.

"Let me introduce you to our ride," Slade said, smoothing his hand over the horse's mane as she nudged her muzzle into his shirt pocket. "This is Nocturne. She knows where I keep the sugar."

Somehow the idea of Slade carrying sugar cubes in his pocket went against her image of him as an unfeeling, cold-hearted cowboy. Clearly his horse, at least, liked him, and that was saying something. Animals sensed when a human was the genuine article, didn't they? Or maybe he just bribed Nocturne with sweets.

Slade checked the cinch. "You about ready to climb up here?"

Laney hesitated, then nodded. Mounting would be awkward with her rounded belly. Getting her foot into the stirrup would be next to impossible, but at least she'd changed into a pair of jeans before she'd left for her walk. It would have been considerably more awkward had she still been in the dress she'd been wearing earlier in the day.

She reached for the saddle horn, intending to attempt to slip her foot in the stirrup, but she never had the opportunity. Before she knew what was happening, Slade's hands spanned her waist—or where her waist would have been seven months ago—and picked her up as if she weighed nothing. His touch was surprisingly gentle as he placed her onto the saddle.

"Are you gonna be more comfortable riding side-saddle or do you think you want to sling your leg over?"

Laney weighed his question in her mind. In her present condition, sitting on a horse *period* wasn't the ultimate in luxury, but as to how she would ride—she supposed that had to do with a number of other factors, such as where, exactly, Slade intended to sit when he joined her. If, in fact, Nocturne could handle the extra burden of the two of them riding together. Slade wasn't a small man.

She pictured herself being relegated to the "back-seat" behind the saddle, clutching her arms around Slade's waist and hanging on for dear life as he galloped home. Then again, if she was in front and he rode behind her, she would by default have those enormous, muscular arms of his wrapped around her. A wave of anxiety rolled over her just thinking about it. She didn't know which would be worse. Certainly neither option even remotely appealed to her.

"I'm walking," he said, answering the question she'd

left unspoken. "So get comfortable. Whatever works for you."

She sighed in relief. One less source of anxiety to deal with—for now. She thought she'd feel more comfortable riding astride so she swung her leg over the saddle horn.

Slade adjusted the stirrups for her height and then waited a beat for her to adjust her weight in the saddle before clicking his tongue to Nocturne. He strode forward without giving Laney so much as another glance. She noted that he followed the fence line, which would have been a good idea for her, as well. Assuming she'd found the fence in the first place. And even then she wouldn't have known which direction to follow it. Still, it was something to keep in mind should she decide to wander off by herself again.

She tried to observe the countryside, to look for landmarks she could use on future outings, but there was nothing to hold her interest and her gaze kept returning to Slade. Thick black hair curled from under the brim of his hat. His broad shoulders sloped into a well-muscled back which then narrowed to a trim waist. He had the build of a perfect athlete and moved like one, too, his stride long and energetic, and yet with the easy country swagger that had clearly melted many ladies' hearts.

Too bad his mouth and his attitude went along with that easy-on-the-eyes profile. Laney pitied the women who'd tried to take Slade on.

Thankfully, he didn't realize she was staring at him. He appeared completely oblivious even to her presence, walking and whistling softly as if he were alone on the grassy plain. He held Nocturne's reins in a loose grip but it was clear his horse would have followed him anyway, lead or not.

Sugar. It was the sugar.

Laney estimated they'd been heading back toward the house for about ten minutes when she first noticed the sky turning into a watercolor painting of pastel pinks and blues, with hues of yellow and orange undertones mixed into a breathtaking combination. The most gifted painter ever born could not have duplicated such a sight, and Laney offered a silent prayer of thanks to the Lord for His handiwork.

Even as she breathed *amen*, she realized the flaw in Slade's rescue strategy. While he'd thankfully saved her from the embarrassment of riding with her, he'd overlooked one important detail.

"I appreciate you helping me out this afternoon," she said, flinching both at the echo of her own voice breaking the silence and the fact that in all honesty she'd much rather have had nearly anybody in the world discover her. "But how is it that you think walking me home is any better than if I'd simply made the hike myself? It appears to me that we're still going to get caught in the dark either way."

He grunted and tossed a condescending look over his shoulder.

"What?"

"I'm bigger than you are."

Seriously? "And that would relate to what I just asked you…how?"

"My stride. It's much longer than yours. Quicker, too, I'd imagine, given your condition. We're going to get there faster than if you were walking on your own.

In fact, we've almost arrived. You'll be able to see the Becketts' house in just a few minutes."

Laney scoffed and shook her head. She didn't see how Slade could make a ridiculous claim like that and make it sound like a fact. Yes, they were still following the fence line, but the fence—and the land—all looked the same. How could he possibly tell where they were in relation to the house?

"You sound mighty sure of yourself."

"I am."

Even though Slade couldn't see her, she rolled her eyes. Exasperating man.

"You didn't even know where you were going, Lancy. You would have wandered around in circles all night."

Point taken. But he didn't have to rub it in.

"And you've got to watch out for Brody's kid."

As if he had to remind her. Feeling as if he'd just jabbed at her, she instinctively laid a protective hand across her belly. She didn't like the way he'd just referred to her precious unborn child as the *kid*. And *Brody's* kid, as if she had no part in the baby at all.

"Stop," she hissed as her anger escalated. Heat expanded through her chest and pressed into her head.

He turned and removed his hat, dabbing sweat from his brow with the sleeve of his shirt. "What?"

"Before we get back to the ranch house, I want to make something perfectly clear to you."

His shoulders visibly tightened and he frowned. "And that would be?"

"Brody's parents have been through enough grief without you making unfeeling remarks about their grandchild. This baby is bringing hope, peace, and—pray God—maybe eventually even a little happiness into their lives. I won't have you upsetting them with your thoughtless implications."

One side of his mouth ticked. She didn't know if that meant she'd gotten through to his hard heart or if it was a sign of anger, but frankly, she didn't care, as long as he agreed to her nonnegotiable terms. She wouldn't have him upsetting the Becketts. Not for anything.

"Well?" she challenged when he didn't speak.

His dark brows lowered over his blue eyes, which had darkened from bright and electric to a midnight color. He glowered at her, and between the scowl and the frown were menacing, almost dangerous overtones. He wasn't a man to cross.

She stared him down, refusing to give in to her roiling stomach and hammering heart. This was one battle she had to win.

"Okay," he growled and forcefully jamming his hat on his head. "I won't say anything negative about you or the baby to the Becketts."

"Do I have your word on that?" She had no idea why she was pressing him. What good was his word, anyway? From what she knew of him, he'd say or do anything to get what he wanted.

He jerked his head in a clipped nod and stalked away from her, causing Nocturne to jolt forward. Thankfully she'd been holding on to the saddle horn or she might have been unseated. The thoughtless man didn't even consider the consequences to his actions. And yet he had the gall to be all over her about hers?

Slade had better not renege on his promise, if he knew what was good for him. Because if he somehow hurt Brody's parents—well, he'd have her to deal with.

And it wouldn't be pretty.

Chapter Two

Slade uncinched Nock's saddle and slid it from her back, slinging it over a barrel with an audible huff and probably more force than was strictly necessary. Since he was temporarily taking over some of Brody's duties for the Becketts, he'd recently been stabling Nocturne in their barn and not at his parents' spread next door, where Slade usually kept her. His two brothers ran the family ranch, leaving him to pursue his own interests.

In his day job he was a member of Serendipity's police force, and he stayed busy with the local small-town rodeo circuit on the weekends. Maybe someday he'd have a ranch of his own, when he settled down. *If* he settled down. But he was having too much fun being an unabashed bachelor to think about that day.

Or at least he had been, until Brody's death. Slade no longer considered himself a carefree bachelor. That life had little appeal to him now. Not without Brody. The importance of living every day to its full value meant more than ever.

He should never have given his word that he wouldn't talk to the Becketts about the baby Laney was carrying and his suspicion that she might take advantage of them, or worse yet, not stick around once the baby had been born, take off again as she'd done right after the funeral. Brody's folks were like second parents to him, and he wouldn't forgive himself if they ended up getting hurt when he could have said or done something to keep themselves from heartache. He didn't know what Laney's game was, but there were too many unanswered questions that left Slade wary of her motives. In their grief, it made perfect sense that Grant and Carol Beckett would be quick to grasp at a carrot like the one Laney was dangling before them.

A grandchild. Brody's legacy. A flesh-and-blood reminder of their son.

Slade winced as pain jolted sharply through his chest. He couldn't wrap his mind around it. What kind of world did he live in where a good man was taken away just as a new life was given?

Why Brody? He'd been a far better man that Slade could ever hope to be. And now to find out that Brody would have been a father. It was almost too much to bear. Why was he still here when Brody was gone? Where was God in all this?

Slade brushed Nock's sweat-soaked back with long, even strokes. It didn't make sense. Brody had only recently given his heart to God, vowed to change his ways, and yet had never been allowed to see that through. He'd never been able to go home to Laney and make a new start. He'd never even known he was about to be a father.

Slade had likewise made a commitment to God, for all the good it had done him. After nearly a year of living his new faith, he was more aware than ever that he was too rough a man to settle down and be *good*. Not like what he figured God expected of him. It wasn't fair.

Brody—he would have made it. He could have become the man God wanted him to be—with a wife and a family. Brody would have managed to change his life completely, and for the better, if it weren't for Slade goading him into riding Night Terror that one last time at the rodeo. Bring home the purse, Slade had told Brody, and Laney would be sure to forgive him for whatever fight had caused their split. In truth, Slade hadn't cared about Brody using the money to placate Laney. It had really been just one man's thrill-seeking challenge to another. It made him sick just to think about it.

If he hadn't taken that ride, if he hadn't gone for that prize, Slade had no doubt Brody would have managed to patch things up with his estranged wife without the insubstantial purse a small-town rodeo afforded. Surely Laney wouldn't have wanted to separate her baby from his or her daddy. Brody would have been the best father ever to that little baby Laney was carrying.

He would have been so happy. So pleased.

It was painfully easy for Slade to picture the joy Brody would have found in a son or daughter, the proud papa holding his infant in his arms for the first time. Teaching his kid to ride a horse and rope a cow, raising up a new generation of Becketts to work the land that had been in their family for over a century.

Now—nothing.

The child would grow up without knowing his or her father. Without having Brody's fine influence to emulate.

And Slade could have prevented that loss. All of it.

He smothered the curse that came naturally to his lips—a bad habit that was difficult to break, but he was trying. God forgive him, swearing was the least of his sins.

He dumped a bucket of oats into Nock's bin and made sure she had plenty of fresh water. When he was finished, out of habit more than anything else, he headed for the Becketts' ranch house. He'd gone about twenty feet when he stopped so suddenly his boots created a cloud of dust from the dirt path. His breath turned as heavy in his chest as if he'd run several miles. Sweat dotted his brow despite the cool evening and he dabbed at it with the corner of his shirt.

Things were different now—and if Laney stuck around, they always would be. The easy camaraderie he shared with Grant and Carol, folks he considered as second parents to him, would be history. Slade was a living, walking reminder of all they had lost—in addition to being a man Laney had despised from the start, long before his thoughtless dare had cost her a husband. Why should they want to have anything to do with him when instead they would have Brody's baby to love?

Maybe he shouldn't visit the Becketts tonight. It would probably be better for all concerned if he just turned around and walked away. If it wasn't enough that he might cause Grant and Carol any means of distress, he and Laney had knocked heads enough times already for one day.

Then again, why should he let Laney dictate anything he did with his life? If he wanted to visit with the Becketts, he'd do it, Laney or no. Grant and Carol hadn't given him any reason to believe his presence caused them any grief, although now that he thought about it, he would try to be more aware of their feelings.

His decision made, he hastened to the house. He didn't go to the front door as a guest might do, but rather entered through the mudroom like one of the family, where he removed his boots and hung his hat on a peg on the wall and then washed up in the sink, using extra soap and scrubbing thoroughly to make sure his hands were clean, then wiping his face clean with a nearby towel. Carol Beckett would have his hide if he got dirt on her good rugs or touched her furnishings with grubby hands.

"Slade." Grant Beckett emerged from the kitchen and extended his hand for a firm shake. "Good to see you, son. Join us in the kitchen. Carol's making cookies, and you know how she gets when she starts baking. She's already made enough baked goods to feed a small army."

"Be happy to take a few off your hands, sir."

"Thought you would." Grant slapped Slade's back affectionately.

Slade entered the kitchen and immediately tensed when he saw Laney propped on a stool next to the counter, laughing at something Carol had said. They looked like a couple of giggly schoolgirls with their heads close together, sharing secrets.

His gut churned and he frowned, remembering the promise he'd made to Laney. Once again he wished he wouldn't have made it, if only for the fact that he could use some advice right now—like what part he might be able to play in giving Brody's baby everything he or she deserved. What he could do for the child.

Brody's baby.

There it was again, glaring before him, as clear and bright as looking straight at the midday sun. The inherent happiness in Laney's brown eyes and the way she shared that pleasure with Carol—the *knowing*. The anticipation. The joy.

Brody's baby.

A link to his friend that went far beyond words or memories. Slade swallowed hard against the emotions pummeling him.

Laney's presence wasn't doing the Becketts any harm, he realized. Not now. Not until she up and left town, which Slade was fairly certain she would do. The real danger wasn't that she'd upset them now, but that she'd abandon them later. How would Carol and Grant feel when their status as grandparents—their only living link with their beloved son—was relegated to some back burner so Laney could move on to the next thing in her life? She'd split with Brody fast enough when he didn't fall into line with her silly expectations even though she'd claimed to love him. How much easier would it be for her to walk away from his parents?

The mixture of grief and excitement he'd experienced only moments earlier was quickly replaced by a panic that made his pulse roar in his ears. As bad as he felt for Grant and Carol at the thought of them losing access to their grandchild, there was yet another reason for him to worry.

What if *he* had no part in the baby's life?

Personally, he thought she was a pain in the neck, but when other people looked at her, they probably saw Laney as a young, attractive woman. She'd won Brody's heart, after all. She was bound to meet a man, get married again and settle down far away from Serendipity.

Brody would be nothing more to her than a sad, distant memory, one she'd likely tuck into the back of her mind as she moved on with her life. It hurt his heart just to think about it.

"There's the man of the hour." Carol beamed at him as she passed him a plate piled with warm oatmeal cookies. "I understand we owe you a debt of gratitude."

"I'm sorry?" he asked with a confused glance toward Carol and then to Grant. Man of the hour? Gratitude? What were they talking about?

"Heard tell you rescued our princess from danger today." Grant grinned at him and wagged his eyebrows.

Still unable to decipher what they were talking about, Slade's gaze flashed to Laney, but she only rolled her eyes and shrugged.

They were talking about Laney?

Princess?

Yeah, right. Laney was a regular damsel in distress. And that would make him—what? Prince Charming? A knight in shining armor? The Becketts were barking up the wrong tree with that one. He scoffed at the nonsensical notion.

"There he goes," Carol said, nodding her head as if she'd disclosed some major secret. "I told you he was going to make light of his actions. He never admits the good he does. Has to maintain that tough cowboy image, you know. Never lets on that there's a kind heart underneath that gruff exterior."

Slade barked out a laugh and everyone joined him. Whatever else he could be accused of, and there was plenty, making himself into something he wasn't was not even on the list. And kindness wasn't something he was often accused of, either.

"Laney would have been fine," he assured the Becketts. Maybe that wasn't entirely accurate, but he didn't want them making too much of his actions, which hadn't been entirely altruistic. "She just got a little turned around. I'm sure she would have found the fence and made it back to the house with no problem. Please. It's no big deal."

"Maybe. Maybe not," Carol said, shaking her head. "But I'm grateful all the same, and so is Laney."

He very much doubted *gratitude* was what Laney was feeling for him. Not from the frown she flashed at him when she thought the Becketts weren't looking.

Slade bit into a cookie and groaned with pleasure. His own mother didn't cook a lick, and since there was no other woman with a constant presence in his life, the only fresh baked goods he ever got besides Carol's occasional but heartfelt forays into baking were Phoebe Hawkins's fare from Cup O' Jo's Café in town. Phoebe was a professional chef and her baked goods were delicious, but they lacked the significance of being baked just for him, with love.

He poured himself a tall glass of ice-cold milk and took a long drink, then wiped his lips with the back of his hand to prevent a milk mustache. He caught Laney's gaze and she lifted a brow.

What? Was she laughing at him?

"You've never heard of milk and cookies?"

She smirked. "You've utterly ruined your tough-guy cowboy image for me, you know."

He shrugged, trying to make light of her comment, even if it was a direct strike to his ego. "Don't knock it until you try it." He met her gaze, speaking without words. *Or knock me when you don't even know me.*

She glared right back at him, and her gaze was no less telling. It stated clearly that she knew him well enough to judge him and find him wanting.

"Consider the cookies and milk the least we can do as your reward for a job well done," Carol said, grinning mischievously and seeming completely oblivious to the silent war brewing between her two guests.

"If I'm going to get cookies and milk every time I'm good, you can count on me to rescue fair damsels every day of the week."

He was joking, of course, and the Becketts chuckled along with him, but instead of joining in the laughter, Laney frowned.

"I am neither fair nor a damsel in distress," Laney remarked. Slade wondered if Carol and Grant could hear the ice in her tone or if she only sounded cold to him.

Apparently he was the only one who'd interpreted her frostiness because if anything, Carol's eyes sparkled not with surprise, but with *concern* for the woman. "We're just grateful you're here with us, Laney. We only wish the circumstances were better."

Laney's expression fell and for a moment even Slade felt sorry for her. She looked thoroughly devastated at the reminder of Brody's death. He'd known his fair share of female deceit in his life, but could a woman fake that kind of pain?

"Speaking of," Slade inserted, seeing an opening to ask what was really on his mind. Maybe it was wrong of him to take advantage of the moment, given Laney's current vulnerability, but he wasn't sure how else to bring up the subject. It was now or never. "How long are you staying, Laney?"

Hmmph. So much for casual. He couldn't have sounded

worse if he'd tried. Every eye in the room turned on him in surprise. He wished he had figured out a more tactful way to ask the question, but he was as good at being tactful as the proverbial bull in a china shop, bumping around and smashing things—feelings—with his words.

"Didn't she tell you?" Grant asked, scratching his red-blond beard. "She's staying in Serendipity for good. This is Laney's permanent home now."

As a matter of fact, she hadn't mentioned anything about her future plans, not that he had asked. He was relieved to hear it all the same. How else would he be able to be a part of Baby Beckett's life?

Of course, that meant he'd have to deal with Laney on a regular basis. But he'd do what he had to do. The baby was that important to him.

"Nice of you to give her somewhere to stay for now," he acknowledged. She'd probably be looking for a place of her own soon. Maybe he could help her find something, extend the olive branch, so to speak.

"Oh, no." Carol shook her head, her white curls bobbing. "You misunderstand. It's the other way around. It's nice of *her* to give *us* a place to stay."

"What?" Slade's pulse roared in his ears and his voice rose. His gut turned wildly and lurched in nauseating waves. "What are you talking about?"

"Brody never told you?" The depth and restraint in Carol's tone suggested Slade had better calm down before speaking again. He recognized the *mother* tone of her voice when he heard it and took it as the warning it was. He inhaled deeply, trying to calm the whirlwind in his mind.

"Sorry," he muttered, though he wasn't really feeling it. He stared at the ground as if a hole would open and swallow him, which might be the better way to get out of this sticky situation. "I shouldn't have raised my voice. You just caught me off guard."

Which was the understatement of the century.

Carol rolled cookie dough balls in her palms as if it was every day that she said things to him that turned his whole world upside down and backward. "It's in the will. Black and white, just as we expected it to be. There are no surprises here, Slade. Brody left everything to Laney." She smiled at him without an ounce of anxiety or regret showing in her features, and then her warm, compassionate gaze shifted to Laney. "She owns this ranch, part and parcel."

If glowering were an art form, Slade McKenna would have made a million dollars out of it. At the moment, his face was an alarming shade of red, almost as if he were being choked with the effort of holding his temper in check. He clenched his fists into tight knots and Laney could see his pulse hammering in the tense lines of his neck. She didn't even want to know what was running through his mind right now, but she suspected she was about to find out.

"Brody. Left. Her. Everything?" He separated each word into its own unique sentence, each one with more emphasis, more power, than the last.

Laney felt the unfathomable urge to duck beneath the counter to avoid the coming explosion. Clearly Slade was doing everything in his power to contain his words, but she had little faith in his self-control. He was too much like Brody, only more volatile in temper. Just as recklessly, foolishly impulsive, with no restraint. If he

was this angry, then sooner or later—likely sooner—
he'd snap.

The prospect was distinctly unsettling. The man was
downright scary in his current state. He looked completely mad, poised to snort and kick in every direction.

But no matter how she was quaking on the inside,
she didn't allow herself to do so much as flinch. She
wouldn't give him the pleasure of knowing he had affected her in any way, much less that he had intimidated her. She straightened her spine and squarely met
his gaze, ready for whatever fireworks were about to
explode.

Except they didn't.

He was clearly affected by the news that she was the
new owner of the ranch. He glared at her. He swept in
a long, ragged breath and tunneled his fingers through
his dark hair.

But he didn't yell. Didn't fume.

In fact, he didn't say a word.

His reaction—or lack thereof—was far more fright-
ening to Laney than if he'd ranted and raved. The fact
that he could contain his emotions suggested an entirely
unexpected strength of character. The thought would
be more comforting if that strength didn't seem so focused on hating her.

His eyes were spitting fire, his gaze accusing her of
a myriad of offenses.

She tipped her chin, unwilling to give him an inch
in this silent war of wills. She had no reason to back
down. He was the one making all of the incorrect assumptions here, not that she needed to explain herself
to him. She'd done nothing wrong.

Anyway, it was none of his business.

"I don't understand. How was the ranch Brody's to give?" Slade's gaze shifted to Carol, and Laney observed the immediate change in his demeanor. Tempered. Respectful. Deferential. Everything he *wasn't* whenever he spoke to her. "Not to put too fine a point on it, but doesn't the ranch belong to the two of you? I guess I just assumed—"

Grant held up a hand to staunch Slade's flow of words. Slade actually looked relieved that he hadn't had to finish his sentence. As well he should be.

"We aren't getting any younger," Grant explained in a no-nonsense tone. "We spoke to Brody about the ownership of the ranch right after we found out he'd married Laney. He told us he was planning on raising a family here. It seemed only right to pass the reins along while we were still alive to see it."

Slade winced visibly and Laney wondered what he was thinking.

Carol moved to Laney's side and placed one arm around her shoulders and her opposite hand on Laney's belly. It would have bothered Laney had a stranger been so intimate, but she already considered Carol a mother to her. "And now you can see just how right we were to make that call when we did. We couldn't possibly have known about the baby at the time, but the good Lord had it safe in His hands. Now Brody's family will be able to live and thrive on this ranch. It isn't quite the way we envisioned it, but—" Carol's voice cut out with emotion "—at least Laney and the baby will have the ranch to help get them by."

"What about y'all?" His question was directed to Carol and Grant but his eyes were on Laney.

She hated how Slade was able to make her feel as if

she'd done something wrong when she hadn't. He had no right to even think such negative things about her, never mind hint his suspicions aloud. She had left a perfectly good career in business management at a large marketing firm in order to honor Brody's memory and raise his son or daughter the way Brody would have wanted. In the country. On the land. Did Slade imagine she would heartlessly throw Brody's parents to the curb after all that?

The Becketts were already family to her, and as dear to her heart as her own mother and father. They had welcomed her and embraced both her and her unborn child. They had never once questioned her relationship with their son, as complicated as that had been. She was perfectly aware she owed them more than she could ever repay.

But she would, of course, give them every courtesy she could to make their lives easier in any way she was able. So why did she feel the need to justify herself to Slade?

"Laney has been nothing but kind," Carol assured Slade, her tone brooking no argument from him.

"I'm sure she has been," he responded, sounding as if he believed exactly the opposite. "But still—you have to understand why I'd be worried about your future."

Only the fact that Slade sounded genuinely concerned about the Becketts kept Laney from pelting something at him. He seemed to be missing the point— or rather, *all* of the points. It was high time to set him straight.

"There's nothing to worry about. Grant and Carol are staying right here. I may technically own the ranch, but in a very real way they have taken me in when I needed them most. I can never begin to repay their generosity, but I'm certainly going to try."

Slade brushed his palm across the stubble on his jaw and gave Laney's belly a pointed look. He appeared to be debating something in his mind.

She tensed, ready for the worst he could give.

His gaze shifted to Carol. Without warning, he strode forward and enveloped the older woman in a big, affectionate bear hug, dwarfing Carol and causing her to giggle like a young girl. "You know I love you both."

Laney nearly fell off her stool. Of everything Slade could have said or done, verbally and physically expressing his love for this family was the last possible guess she would have made. Who would have imagined that the harsh, judgmental cowboy Laney was familiar with had a soft side? Clearly he held great affection for the Becketts, and to her very great surprise, he wasn't afraid to express it.

"If y'all are set on accepting Laney into your lives, then I will, too. I'll show her around the ranch and give her some pointers on country living. She's got a huge learning curve here, and I'm sure she can use all the help she can get."

Laney sniffed indignantly. That was all well and good for Mr. Arrogant, assuming she would be doing back flips because he'd conceded to allow her to live in her own home, and had, in fact, offered to *help* her, whatever that meant.

As if she needed his assistance—with *anything*. He made it sound as if he was doing her a favor. It obviously never even occurred to the big lug that she might not want anything to do with him. As if it was his decision to make whether or not she was part of his life. No need to ask her what *she* thought about it.

Even if she wasn't seven months pregnant, she would in no way be doing any kind of gymnastics over Slade McKenna. Hadn't he already created enough havoc in her life? Hadn't he stuck his nose into her business when he had no right to be there and ultimately been the primary cause of the demise of her marriage? Hadn't he led Brody down all the wrong paths, tempting him with all manner of reckless ideas when Brody most needed to learn to be responsible and to live up to his commitments?

Laney wanted nothing to do with him. Not one single thing.

But when Slade raised his milk glass in a silent toast to her, she realized just how difficult it was going to be to avoid him and all his meddling in her affairs. The Becketts accepted what he said at face value. They clearly adored him, and he filled an extra special role in their lives now that Brody was gone.

Whether she liked or not—and she didn't, not one bit—it appeared Slade was about to become a permanent part of her life.

Chapter Three

Slade awoke in a cold sweat, thrashing back and forth as he wrestled with the blanket that had somehow become knotted around his ankles. In his mind he kept hearing the eight-second buzzer—a bull rider's favorite sound and now his worst nightmare.

He groaned and yanked at the stubborn blanket, refusing to let his thoughts go back to the moment that had darkened his life permanently. Unfortunately, his life was about to get even more cloudy, with the distinct possibility of thunderstorms in his near future.

He had a new goal in life, a new mission to fill his time and his thoughts. He had a baby to protect.

If that meant being in the company of Laney Beckett, then so be it. A restless night's sleep hadn't made the situation any more palatable, but at least he knew what he should be doing next—getting Laney under Dr. Delia's care. Hopefully she'd been seeing a doctor all along, taking extra precautions to make sure she and the baby were healthy, but she was here in Serendipity now and Slade trusted Delia, whom he'd grown up with, more than any city doctor he'd ever encountered.

Besides, if Laney was sticking around like she said she was going to do, Dr. D. would likely be the one delivering Brody's baby.

Might as well start out the way he intended to finish—making sure Brody's kid had the best of everything life could offer. He took a shower and then made a quick phone call as he dressed. It took a bit of finagling, but he managed to get Laney an appointment for late morning as he'd hoped.

His beat-up blue pickup truck rumbled to a start and within minutes he was pulling into the Becketts' long driveway. Located only a few miles out of Serendipity proper, the Becketts' ranch bordered Slade's folks' spread, which had been one of the many reasons he and Brody had originally become friends. Slade's two older brothers still worked the land, but Slade had opted to become a cop and live in an apartment complex just off Main Street.

Once he arrived at the ranch, he parked next to a pathetic little silver hybrid, which he assumed was Laney's. Certainly Grant and Carol would never drive anything so small and impractical. There were more dirt roads than paved ones in Serendipity, especially outside of town. Her ridiculous little car wouldn't handle the washboard more than a dozen times before breaking down, and he shuddered to think of her driving that flimsy car in a rainstorm.

Slade scoffed and shook his head. The woman now owned a ranch and she drove a hybrid vehicle. What kind of irony was that? She clearly didn't have the first clue about country living. Leave it to Laney to make all the wrong choices. She really *did* need his help if she was going to have any hope of making it here.

He rapped twice on the Becketts' front door to announce himself and then entered without waiting for anyone to answer. He knew Grant and Carol were both early risers, and if Laney wasn't an early bird then she needed to learn to be. It was part and parcel of life on a ranch. Up with the sun. Starting now.

Instead of encountering Carol and Grant, the first person Slade came upon was Laney. Dressed in garish bright pink sweatpants and a purple sweatshirt that stretched tightly over her middle, she sported rectangular black-framed reading glasses which were perched on the end of her nose, reminding Slade of an owl. Or a librarian. She was stretched out on the living room sofa with a book in her hands.

A romance novel. It figured.

She didn't appear to have heard him enter the house, or else she was too engrossed in her novel to care. Or maybe she was just ignoring him.

"Hey," he said, his voice still low and hoarse from sleep. He cleared his throat and waited for her to acknowledge him.

She raised her glasses and glanced up at him, then rolled her eyes and sighed loudly. "Oh, lovely. What are you doing here?"

"Well, good morning to you, too."

She picked up a mug from a nearby end table and took a noisy sip of the contents. "Can we start over? I'm not a human being until after my second cup of coffee."

He frowned. It was a good thing he was here to take her to see the doctor, if she was loading herself up with caffeine. He didn't know the first thing about pregnancy, but he was fairly certain coffee wasn't good for her.

"Should you be drinking coffee? Isn't that bad for Brody's baby?"

Her eyebrows rose as if he'd said something shocking and not simply suggested she take better care of herself and the baby. "It's just an expression. If you must know, I'm drinking tea this morning."

He opened his mouth for the obvious follow-up question, but she held up a hand to stave off his words.

"Decaffeinated green tea, full of antioxidants that are *good* for Baby Beckett. Are you always this pushy?"

He started to shake his head but ended up shrugging a shoulder. "Sometimes."

When it had to do with the welfare of Brody's baby.

"Well, cut it out. You'll quickly discover I don't respond to bossiness And I don't like bullies."

Was she calling him a bully again? She'd probably be surprised to know he was the guy in high school who championed the little guys. *He* wasn't a bully—he was the guy who beat up the bullies of the world.

Sooner or later, she'd realize that she couldn't be more wrong about him. But he didn't have time to argue about it with her now. They needed to get going if they were going to be on time for the appointment.

"Get up. Get dressed. I've come to take you to the doctor."

"I don't have an appointment. I'm sure you're aware I've been pretty busy since I arrived in Serendipity. I haven't even had the chance to go online and find a local OB."

"Serendipity only has one doctor, and she does everything from patching up skinned knees to delivering babies. That's why I made an appointment for you."

She'd been about to take another sip of tea, but at

Slade's pronouncement she sputtered and then inhaled the liquid, sending her into a fit of coughing.

Not knowing quite how to help her but wanting to do something productive, Slade crouched by her side and patted her back.

"Cut it out," she said when she could speak. She squirmed away from him. "Stop hitting me."

He dropped to his knees in surprise, leaning his hands on his thighs. "I wasn't hitting you," he protested, appalled by the very suggestion that he would hit a woman. "You were choking, and I was trying to—"

"Give me the Heimlich maneuver? Knock the breath out of my lungs?"

He scowled. The least she could do was show a little bit of gratitude, but no. She was ridiculing him, pressing down on his male ego, which was aching to spring back into action and snap back at her.

"My tea went down the wrong pipe," she informed him, pursing her lips. "I didn't need your help, thank you. Now, what is this about making me a doctor's appointment?"

He clenched his jaw. He was about to tell her to forget the whole thing, seeing as she didn't think she needed his *help*, but he couldn't very well turn his back on Brody's baby, no matter how downright crazy the kid's mother made him.

"You happen to be especially blessed today," he informed her, not caring if his tone was cold. She was lucky he didn't just walk out right now. "Since Dr. D. is the only doctor in town, she's usually booked for weeks in advance, barring emergencies. Providentially, she had a cancellation for this morning. I convinced her to take that time to see you."

Laney's brow lowered. She appeared undecided. "I do need to be under a doctor's care for the duration of my pregnancy," she admitted, sounding as if she were saying the words against her better judgment.

Her expression was cringe-worthy, and once again Slade experienced the strong urge to simply get up and walk away. She didn't need to look as if she was getting a tooth pulled when he was doing her a favor.

"You need to get dressed, then," he reminded her. "We have a half hour before we have to be there for your appointment. It's only a five minute drive to Main Street where her office is located, but I don't know how long it takes you to do—whatever it is that women need to do to be ready to go out."

She laughed. He raised a brow, but she only shook her head.

What had he said that was so funny?

Women. He'd never understand them and, frankly, he didn't even want to try. *Especially this one.*

If it weren't for Brody's baby, he'd be out of there so fast Laney's head would spin. It was asking a lot just for him to be in the same room with her, but for Brody's kid, Slade would grit his teeth and try to get through it.

"I'm a wash and wear kind of girl," she informed him, tossing her hair over her shoulder with an animated flip of her hand which to Slade felt like a major brush-off. "I'll be ready in five. And I'm going to ignore the fact that you just tried to order me around again."

His gaze widened and he hoped he wasn't gaping.

"But don't do it again."

"Baby is growing just exactly like he or she is supposed to be," Delia informed Laney, who breathed a sigh of relief. She had no reason to believe anything was amiss, but it was still nice to know she and the baby were healthy, especially with Slade breathing down her neck. The man simply didn't know when to leave well enough alone.

"You decided not to find out whether it is a boy or girl?" Delia asked as she rolled up her tape measure. "I did the same thing with my son Riley. You don't get too many pleasant surprises in life. Having a baby is one of the best."

"It is," Laney agreed, tears springing to her eyes as grief clenched her chest so severely that she could not catch a breath. This was a surprise she should have been able to share with her husband.

Delia was instantly by her side, gripping her hand. "I am so sorry. That was thoughtless of me. I should never—"

"No. It's fine." Laney laid a tender hand on her belly and felt the baby kick. "At least I have a way to honor Brody. His love continues on through this baby, so how could I ever consider Baby Beckett as anything but a blessing?"

Laney heard a loud thud coming from the waiting room and wondered what Slade was doing that was making so much noise. Probably inadvertently knocking things over with those brawny arms of his like the big boor he was.

The doctor glanced toward the waiting room and chuckled. "Looks like Baby Beckett is not the only blessing in your life. Slade was pretty insistent you get in to see me sooner rather than later. Thought it was important for you to get the care you need, and if you haven't yet noticed, he's pretty persuasive when he needs to be. He's a good friend to have on your side, that one."

Seriously? Delia must be deluded if she thought Slade could be an actual asset as anyone's friend, most especially hers. He wasn't insistent. He was downright pushy. And arrogant. His friendship with Brody had led Brody down a destructive path, one that had virtually destroyed her relationship with her spouse. Even if Brody had lived, Laney wasn't positive her marriage would have survived despite her prayers and her best efforts. Not with Slade's influence on her husband. Despite the hastiness of their marriage, Laney had been committed to the relationship. But Brody—

"I guess he's okay," she conceded when Delia's gaze became curious. *Okay for what* was the real question.

"I imagine he's a little overprotective of you and the baby. He and Brody were very close."

"I know."

"Since they were kids. Those two were inseparable. He took Brody's death hard—harder than most. I think it's good for him to have a positive way to direct his energy, looking after Brody's baby."

Was that what Slade was trying to do? Insinuate himself into her life so he could have an influence on her baby?

That was *so* not going to happen.

As if she would ever subject her child to anything more than a bare minimum of time with a womanizing adrenaline junky whose idea of fun was taking crazy risks with his life. Someone with no stability, not to mention his complete lack of understanding when it came to what romantic relationships were all about. He had less sense than the big, shiny belt buckles he wore.

Not exactly mentor material, and not whom she wanted around her child. She was going to be the best mom she could be to Baby Beckett, and that included avoiding people who clearly wouldn't be good for the child. Nothing Slade tried, either by being his usual overbearing self or by turning his good looks and charm on her, would change her mind. Thankfully, he had not yet tried the catch-more-flies-with-honey tactic with her, but she knew it to be the key weapon in his arsenal, and she suspected if he couldn't win one way, he'd try another.

She'd learned her lesson about falling for easy charm, and she wouldn't make the same mistake again. She'd once made an impulsive leap into a permanent relationship based on little more than a wink and a grin, but she was no longer that young, foolish woman—and she had a baby to protect.

Laney heard another thud in the waiting room and Delia excused herself to go investigate. Moments later, Slade appeared in the doorway, his hat clutched in his hand.

"Is everything all right? You're okay? The kid's doing well?"

If he hadn't sounded so sincere—worried, even—Laney would have rolled her eyes. As it was, she reluctantly answered his question. "I'm fine. We're fine."

To Laney's surprise, he sagged in relief. As if he really cared.

"Did you think there'd be a problem?"

He shook his head and then, as if changing his mind, he shrugged. "Maybe. Didn't know all the particulars. Just wanted to get you checked out."

"Well, consider me checked. Baby is good to go."

When Slade's eyes widened, she added, "But not for two months yet."

He smiled. It was the first time she'd ever seen him smile—at least the genuine article and not the catching-the-eye-of-the-ladies grin he usually sported. Twin dimples carved deeply into his cheeks. On any other guy the dimples would have made him look boyish, but Slade was all man. Which, to Laney, at least, was one of his biggest shortcomings—among many.

"What were you doing that made so much noise out there?"

He shook his head. "Just pacing. The waiting room is too small for comfort."

Or he was too large.

"He's kicking right now," she said, laying a hand against the rib Baby Beckett was currently using as soccer practice and wondering if she should even make this small concession. She suspected Brody would have wanted it, which was the only reason she continued. "Would you like to feel?"

"It's a boy?"

"Oh, no. I mean, I don't actually know—I've chosen not to find out the gender until I give birth. Saying he/she every time I refer to the baby is getting to be too much of a tongue twister. I should probably just stick with Baby Beckett. It's easier to say."

"Yeah," Slade agreed, his voice unusually deep and thick. "You know Brody wouldn't have cared if Baby Beckett was a boy or a girl. He would have loved the baby just the same, no matter what."

"He would have been a good father." Her throat clogged with emotion. Their eyes met, and just for a moment they mutually shared the one thing they had in common.

Grief.

"The best." The corner of Slade's mouth ticked, a tell Laney now recognized as reaction to stress.

"Come here," she urged, holding out her hands.

He looked reticent, almost shy, as he stepped forward and offered her his hand.

She laid his palm where the baby was moving and the child responded with a swift kick, then another.

Slade's brilliant blue eyes filled with wonder. "Well, I'll be."

"Amazing, right?"

"Amazing doesn't even begin to cover it." He shook his head. "It's hard to believe Brody's kid is in there, just waiting to come out and say, 'Hey.'"

Laney chuckled. "I'm not sure that's the first thing Baby Beckett will say. You never know, though. Could be."

One side of his mouth kicked up. "Close enough. Two months, huh?"

"More or less. You do know babies don't necessarily come right on their due dates, right?" She had a clear mental picture of Slade hustling her off to the hospital just because the calendar said the time was right. That was just exactly the sort of thing he would do, exasperating man.

"On their own time, huh?"

"And in their own way. Each baby is different. Their own little person, with a unique personality. One of God's greatest blessings."

She half expected Slade to scoff at her for her beliefs,

but he nodded fervently and curled the brim of his hat in his fist. "The very best of them. Especially this one."

"I wish Brody was here."

Slade's gaze clouded with pain. He might not be the nicest of men, but there was no doubt he'd cared for Brody.

"I'm sorry. I shouldn't keep bringing that up." She couldn't believe she was apologizing to him, but she couldn't seem to help herself.

"No. You're right. Of course Brody should be here." He turned away from her and punched at the air. "He *should* be here. Not me."

What did that even mean? She understood the sentiment but not the anger.

"I'm sure we'll both do our best to honor Brody's memory."

Slade turned back and shoved out a breath. "For Brody. We'll give the baby the best of everything. Enroll him in football. Baseball."

"Ballet lessons," Laney added with a chuckle, feeling a crazy mixture of joy and sorrow. Grief was impossible to understand.

Slade looked surprised, but then he nodded. "Right. If it's a girl. No way are we enrolling any boy of Brody's in dance class."

She didn't know why they were discussing what they would do for Baby Beckett as if these were decisions the two of them would make together. Slade sounded awfully determined to be a part of her child's life.

"Maybe he'll want to take dance."

Slade scoffed. "Let's hope not. Of course, you do realize Brody would have taught his little girls how to throw a football, not to mention rope and ride every bit as well as his sons."

Laney chuckled. "I'd expect no less from him. I'll be spending the rest of my life in Serendipity. I would hope if Baby Beckett is a girl she'll know her way around the ranch."

"I could do it." Slade's statement was made so low she could barely understand the words.

"I beg your pardon?"

"Roping and riding. I could teach the kid how to do that stuff. Boy or girl. Either way. If you wanted me to, I mean."

That was probably the nicest thing Laney had ever heard Slade say. He'd actually asked. Kind of. Or maybe her emotions were overwhelming her. Either way, her answer was the same. It had to be. "I'd like that, and I'm sure Baby Beckett will, as well."

"Good, then. It's settled." His nod was no more than a quick jerk of his chin, his jaw tight and his lips pressed together.

Great. So she'd just sealed the deal. Slade was going to be a part of her child's life for an extended period of time. Maybe always. Which by default meant she'd have to interact with him, as well. How had this conversation gotten so turned around?

"Brody had planned to reconcile with you, you know. Right after the rodeo was finished."

Laney was so startled by the statement she gripped a nearby table for support. She was afraid she'd heard Slade wrong, but when she met his gaze, she knew he'd said just what she'd heard, and for whatever reason was sharing it with her now.

Brody had planned to come home to her.

And then that chance had been taken away from them both.

Chapter Four

Slade's thoughts were a million miles away as he pulled his pickup onto the Becketts' long gravel driveway. Probably a good thing he'd made this very same drive so often over the years, seeing as he couldn't seem to be able to keep his mind on the road.

Even after nearly a week of not seeing her, he was thinking of Laney and Brody and wondering what Baby Beckett would look like. Would the little nipper have Brody's white-blond hair or a rich caramel brown like Laney? Laney's chocolate-brown eyes or Brody's light blue ones?

He had no doubt that any kid with Brody's and Laney's genes was going to be a cutie. However Slade personally felt about Laney, any man with eyes in his head would have to admit she was a real looker, the kind of woman that would cause a man to do a double-take if he passed her on the street. And while Slade had no clue what women found attractive in a man, he knew Brody had never had any trouble catching the ladies' attention. Women had flocked to him, especially buckle bunnies like Laney.

Not that it mattered one way or another what the baby looked like. Slade was going to love the kid—purple, green, blue or otherwise. He would love Baby Beckett, and protect and defend the child against whatever life through at him or her. Teach the kid everything he knew about ranching. About life.

It was the least he could do, since it was his fault the child would be growing up without a father. He owed Brody that much, and more.

Slade scowled when he realized there wasn't a single place to park in front of the Becketts' house. What was the deal? If the Becketts were throwing a party, they'd forgotten to invite him—not that anyone had parties on a Monday morning. He couldn't even take a guess what was really going on.

He pulled farther down the driveway and parked his truck in the only empty spot he could find. His original intention in coming to the Becketts' this morning was to saddle Nocturne, ride her to his parents' spread next door where he would stable her permanently, and afterward walk back for his truck.

He'd been bedding his horse at the Becketts' for long enough, though he still had every intention of helping them out wherever and whenever he could, just as he'd promised. He'd give Laney pointers on ranching and of course he'd be around when Baby Beckett arrived, but at the moment he felt it was time to back off and get a little distance from the situation. For his own good. Every day it seemed he was getting more and more wrapped up in Laney, both in the circumstances they each faced and in the woman herself. Half the time he didn't know whether he was coming or going.

"What's all this?" he muttered to himself, taking

stock of the trucks parked up and down the driveway in front of the house—old, new and everything in between. Some familiar. Most not.

He started toward the house to investigate, then turned when he heard a ruckus coming from the ranchers' bunkhouse, where the wranglers slept and Brody's father kept his office. Grant primarily oversaw the ranch, but Brody had always helped when he was around and as time allowed. Slade knew Brody would have eventually found his way home again, taken over the ranch for good. Started a family.

But now everything had changed. Brody was gone. The ranch belonged to Laney. And there was a long line of scruffy, weathered cowboys, some young and some older than their beat-up trucks appeared to be, winding out of the office and around the bunkhouse.

Slade didn't recognize more than a few of them, and he knew everyone in Serendipity. Something was definitely up, and with the way his stomach was twisting and turning, he was fairly certain he wasn't going to like what he found. He'd learned to trust those inner nudges that he couldn't always explain. Those gut feelings were part of what made him so good at everything he did, from bull riding to serving as a police officer.

He strode across the uneven ground, his boots first crunching against the gravel and then silently sweeping through the long grass. He was going to get to the bottom of this.

Now.

It very well might not be any of his business. Grant probably had it all under control—whatever *it* was. Call it curiosity, or another opportunity to find a way to help the Becketts. He'd know soon enough.

"Hey," one of the younger wranglers protested when he ignored the long line of cowboys and cut through to the door of the office. Slade didn't care if he was breaking the rules, and he especially wasn't concerned over what the other men in the long line thought of him. He wasn't some random cowpoke applying for a job at the ranch. Was that why these men were here? Was Grant doing some hiring? Maybe one of the wranglers had given notice.

He entered the office with a friendly greeting for Grant on his lips, but stopped short in the doorway as if he'd slammed into an invisible force field. Laney was sitting behind Grant's desk with those silly reading glasses of hers perched on the end of her nose. She looked completely out of her element, her hair combed back into a neat ponytail, her cheeks flushed a pretty pink and her full lips curved up at the corners. She looked as neat and fresh as a bouquet of tulips in a room that was anything but. Her appearance was a stark contrast to the rest of her surroundings. Random piles of papers and file folders littered the top of the desk. The smell of sweat and leather permeated the room and lingered in the stale air.

And that was to say nothing of the sloppily-dressed wrangler standing before the desk, dusty hat in hand and one side of his shirt untucked and dangling like a tail at the back of his well-worn blue jeans. The man flashed Slade an irritated frown, which Slade completely ignored. The wrangler didn't worry him. He was far more concerned about Laney's thunderous scowl and the lightning flashing in her brown eyes.

Fire and ice. Everything about the woman was contrary.

"What's going on here?" He could guess, but he wanted to hear it from her. He leaned his shoulder against the door frame and folded his arms across his chest.

Her eyes narrowed and her spine straightened. "Excuse me?"

The lanky wrangler across from Laney turned and faced Slade. "Look, buddy, I don't know who you think you are, but there's an interview goin' on here, and in case you didn't notice, there's a line outside the door. You wanna talk to the missus here, go wait your turn with the rest of the boys."

Slade was many things, but a *boy* he wasn't. He stared the man down for a moment before shifting his gaze to Laney, who didn't quite meet his eyes.

Yep. He knew it. The woman had definitely bitten off more than she could chew. If she ended up hiring some mouthy cowpoke like the guy standing in front of her, there would be no end to the trouble she'd find herself in. The fellow would take advantage of her at every turn. In fact, he was fairly certain most of the cowboys hanging outside the office fell into that category. He couldn't imagine why Grant thought he could leave her alone to handle whatever hiring was being done here. Laney was so far out of her element it wasn't even funny, and he suspected she knew it.

"You," he said, pointing to the cowboy and then jerking his thumb toward the door. "Out."

The man clenched his fists around the brim of his hat and pressed his chest out like a rooster. Slade knew a challenge when he saw one. He stood to his full six-two height and took a single step forward. He didn't need to posture. The warning in his gaze would be enough to send the scrawny man running, if the fellow had any sense.

"This ain't over," the man threatened, jamming his hat on his head before stomping out the door.

"Yeah, whatever." Slade grinned in satisfaction and nodded at Laney. "That guy won't be back."

Laney stood up so fast she knocked a pile of file folders to the floor. "Getting rid of him was *not* your decision to make."

Wait—what?

He'd just saved her the major hassle of having to find a way to boot that guy to the curb. She ought to be thanking him right now. Unless…

"You weren't seriously thinking about—"

Laney cut him off. "No, of course I wasn't. Contrary to what certain people around here believe about me, I do have a brain in my head."

He'd never said—never even *thought*—she was stupid, but she was staring at him as if he'd just openly accused her of that very thing.

No. Not staring.

Glaring daggers at him.

"Are you quite finished trying to take over my interviewing?" she demanded. "Because as you can see from the line outside, I'm super busy right now and I don't have time for your nonsense."

His *nonsense*? Now that was getting personal.

So she didn't want him to stick around. Then forget formalities. He'd cut straight to the chase. If she didn't like it, then too bad for her. He was making this his business now whether she wanted him to or not. She was clearly in over her head, and he wouldn't let her be taken advantage of. "You didn't answer my question.

What are you doing with these guys? Whose position are you looking to fill?"

"Not that it's any of your affair, but I'm looking to hire a foreman." Her brow furrowed and strained lines appeared over her pinched lips.

So she was—what? Cutting Grant off from his own ranch and the only life the man had ever known? And all this after she'd assured him—them—that nothing would change. Anger burned in Slade's gut, rising upward to spread across his shoulder and neck. It was all he could do to keep himself in check.

He should have known better than to trust a woman. To trust Laney.

"Why?" It was the only word he could manage without coming apart on her. He tensed for the answer, ready to be mentally sideswiped and thoroughly prepared to fight back. Baby or no baby, he wasn't going to let Laney step all over Brody's parents. He didn't care what Brody's will said, or what he'd promised the Becketts in regards to Laney. She was not going to get away with this.

"Why?" she repeated, shaking her head. She stared at him with wide, innocent eyes. The woman actually had the gall to look confused, as if she didn't know why he was upset. "Why what? Why I'm hiring a foreman?"

She was trying to play him for a fool. Well, he was having none of it. No woman was going to pull the wool over his eyes, especially not Laney Beckett. She may have fooled Brody, but she'd never get to him.

"Last time I checked, Grant ran this ranch. He's never seen the need to have a foreman before. He's always handled everything himself."

And he didn't need a foreman now. He didn't say the

words aloud. He didn't have to. Clearly Laney understood what was not being said. Good for her. She could read between the lines.

She gave an exasperated sigh. "So that's what this is about. You're worried about the Becketts."

"Yeah, that's what this is about," Slade growled, seething in frustration as he jerked his head toward the doorway. "How am I supposed to take it when I see all those guys out there waiting to take over Grant's life's work?"

With measured steps, Laney returned to her seat behind the desk and gestured to the chair opposite, then leaned down to collect the folders she'd previously knocked to the floor. He, on the other hand, was less smooth in his movements. He stomped to the chair she offered and threw himself into it with a grunt, even going so far as to prop his booted feet on the desktop.

She stared pointedly at his boots and then shook her head, not taking up the bait.

"I'm not trying to hurt Grant," she said, her voice and her gaze softening. "I'm trying to help him."

"By replacing him?" Slade tried to control his tone but knew the question sounded sharp, even judgmental. He couldn't help it, because that was exactly how he was feeling at the moment, and he'd never been very good at masking his emotions.

"I'm not replacing him, exactly. Just finding both of us some extra assistance until I can get my feet under me. He needs more help than I can give him right now, especially until I have the baby. After that, we'll see."

She was talking about Grant as if he was some doddering old senior, not the strong, vibrant rancher who spent every day in the saddle.

"If you think any of that bunch out there can do what Grant does, then you don't know the first thing about running a ranch," Slade said. He would have continued, but Laney cut him off with a frown and a slash of her hand.

"Not that it's any of your business, but you don't need to point out my weaknesses to me. I'm perfectly aware that I have a huge learning curve to conquer." She met his gaze squarely. "And I know I'm not in the best position right now to be taking on ranch work. But make no mistake—I will figure all of this out, even if it takes me a while to get everything straight. I'm determined to do whatever it takes to keep Baby Beckett's legacy on solid ground, so to speak. Nothing and nobody is going to get in my way."

She almost made it sound as if *he* was the one blocking her progress. He bristled. *He* wasn't the one they were talking about right now. "So you're just pushing Grant out of your way?"

Laney looked as if she was about to blow a fuse. He could actually see it in the cherry-red flush of her face. If ever there was a time when he felt like ducking and running for cover, this was it. The woman was ready to explode, and he was the target. "No. Of course not. Nothing remotely like that. I can't even believe you would suggest such a thing. I would never disrespect Grant that way."

"You already have. He doesn't need extra help."

Her gaze locked with his. "Yes, Slade. He does."

"You have no idea what you're talking about. He's spent nearly every day of his life out here working on the ranch."

"Exactly. I'm not saying he's over the hill, but he's

tired. The two of us have talked about it at length. He always assumed Brody would settle down and take responsibility for the ranch some day. Brody passed that duty over to me when he left me the ranch in his will, and I want to do whatever I can to lighten Grant's load. Someday I pray Brody's child will have the honor of taking over this land, but in the meantime, I have every intention of hiring someone knowledgeable to show me the ropes. I've got a long road ahead of me if I'm going to keep the Becketts' cattle business in the black. I need to know every aspect of the business, and I figure a good foreman will be the best way to do that."

"*You're* going to take over running this ranch?" It was one thing to own a ranch—but quite another thing altogether if she thought she could just step in and run the place.

She scoffed. "You don't have to sound so surprised. I'll have you know I have a master's degree in business administration. Granted, I didn't expect my career to lean toward cattle ranching, but I'm fairly certain my background will serve the Becketts in good stead."

He shook his head. "No, I didn't mean—"

"I know exactly what you meant. I have no experience and I'm going to get in way over my head. I won't be able to handle it, and I'm going to crash and burn." Her shoulders stiffened and she rubbed at a spot on her belly.

The baby. In Slade's haste to force the truth from her and find out what was really at the foundation of her actions, he'd forgotten that what affected Laney also affected Baby Beckett. Laney getting all stressed out wasn't going to help Brody's kid, and he didn't want that to happen, no matter how frustrated he was.

She was right about one thing, although probably not in the way she'd meant it. He *didn't* know if she was capable of running a cattle ranch, though he had good reason to doubt it, whether she had one business degree or a dozen. Most folks with ranches were born and raised for country life. He'd only seen her at that one rodeo where she and Brody had met, but as far as Slade knew, Laney had been one of those fancy rodeo princesses who wore lots of sparkles and waved flags around and whose only job was to sit on a horse and look pretty. Which, he granted, she probably did quite well. But she had to realize that wasn't the same thing as wrangling cattle. Not by a long shot.

Even from behind a desk, running a ranch wasn't for the faint of heart. So she had a couple of diplomas hanging on her wall. Good for her. Classroom learning wouldn't cut it, not out here on the range. It was a tough life. It required a firm hand and plenty of understanding of what needed to be done. Even a task as simple as overseeing the wranglers could be a disaster with the wrong person in charge. The interview Slade had walked in on clearly showed that Laney didn't know how to handle those situations. And that was just the tip of the iceberg. There'd be many more challenging and stressful issues she'd have to face.

That was what worried Slade the most. Even if the pressure didn't directly affect the baby, and that was a big *if*—one which Slade didn't want to leave to chance— it would eventually be too much for Laney to handle. If he didn't miss his guess, she'd buckle within a week or two, pack up and leave town for good.

And then where would he be?

Out of Baby Beckett's life.

Slade clenched his jaw to offset the ache that had opened up in his heart. That wasn't going to happen. He couldn't let it happen. No matter what, he had to watch Brody's kid grow up, be part of the kid's life. He needed to be Uncle Slade, the fun one whom the child would look forward to seeing. Baby Beckett was all he had left of his friend, and he would be hog-tied and branded before he let Laney out of his sight and out of his life.

"Send those guys away." He didn't mean for it to sound like a demand, exactly, though he knew that was how it came out.

"Excuse me? Are you trying to order me around again? I believe we've covered this ground already. You don't get to tell me what to do."

He sighed deeply, using every resource in his small arsenal to keep his cool with her. "I'm not giving you an order. I'm trying to help you here, and it would be really good if you'd just listen to what I'm trying to tell you is going to happen."

Her jaw dropped, her gaping mouth only slightly wider than her eyes.

He took a deep breath and started again.

"You can send them away now, and good riddance to every last one of 'em. You don't need to worry about this anymore, and you definitely don't need the hassle of trying to work with any of those guys." He didn't even want to think about what kind of situation she'd almost put herself in. Judging by the looks of them— not to mention by the attitude of the one he'd spoken to himself—none of the wranglers waiting to interview with Laney came even close to what she needed right now. "If you'd rather, I would be happy to do the honors for you, only I'm warning you it won't look so pretty if I'm the one to kick them out."

Her mouth snapped shut and she shook her head. "Really, Slade? Clearly you haven't heard a word I've said all day."

"Oh, I heard, all right. Giving Grant a break. Business degree. Running the ranch." He ticked off the list on his fingers. "But you aren't going to need to interview any more of these wranglers to find someone to show you the ropes. Simple as that."

She huffed out a disbelieving breath and arched one dark eyebrow.

"And why is that?" Her voice sounded more than a little bit acerbic. As if she didn't know what he was talking about.

Oh, maybe she *didn't* know what he was talking about.

Well. He could fix that.

He stood and braced his hands on the desk, leaning forward until his face was mere inches from hers, so close he could smell the fresh, clean woodsy scent of her perfume. Not that he noticed.

"Because," he said softly, slowly, with every ounce of determination and certainty he possessed, "I'm your man."

Miserable man.

Laney took the long way to the community stable in town where Slade had told her to meet him, enjoying a brisk walk to clear her head before heading in the direction he'd indicated. She couldn't imagine why he'd need to spend any time at a public stable, much less why he'd want her to meet him there. Even before he'd agreed to help her learn the ins and outs of the ranching business, he had kept Nocturne on at the Becketts. No need to rent a horse, or find a place to ride one.

If he was planning to start educating her about life on her ranch, she would have thought that he'd want to meet her *at* her ranch.

Slade was her man.

Ugh. Two days wasn't enough time for her to get over his incredible arrogance. She hadn't liked the statement when he'd made it, and she didn't like it now. She was beginning to believe no amount of time would diminish the intensity of the utter annoyance she experienced every time she thought of the stubborn cowboy. Slade was every bit as overbearing in personality as he was in size, and that said a lot, big oaf that he was. If she had any sense at all, she ought to have told him where to hang his offer—right off his beak.

She should have. And she would have.

Except for one tiny, indelible fact which she couldn't ignore even if she wanted to—and oh, how she wanted to.

He was right.

As much as she hated to admit it, Slade showing her the ropes and helping her out until she learned all the things she needed to know to keep the Beckett ranch running smoothly made sense—in the worst possible way. And not only because she'd gotten a bad feeling from every one of the wranglers she had interviewed. Hiring any of them would have been a disaster. She couldn't have trusted a single one of them. And while she couldn't really trust Slade to be kind or compassionate or anything other than the overbearing boor that he was, she knew he had the best interests of the ranch at heart.

He was a friend of the family. For reasons she couldn't even begin to understand, Grant and Carol trusted him implicitly and practically considered him their own son. It was no doubt a great consolation to them to have him around now that Brody was gone. Slade had worked the Beckett land with Brody when they'd been younger, giving him a unique advantage when it came to showing her the ropes.

Hadn't he been checking their fences for the Becketts her first day back in Serendipity? She hated to admit she needed help, most especially from Slade, but his arrival that day had been a Godsend. He'd returned her to the Becketts' house without incident when otherwise she might have—*probably* would have, if she was being honest—been hopelessly lost.

That didn't make it easier for her now. She had to swallow gall just to consider what she was about to do.

Even though she was already feeling winded from the extra weight she carried in her midsection and the way the baby pressed up on her lungs, she picked up her pace to just short of a jog. She missed being able to exercise the way she used to prepregnancy. She'd been a regular jogger. Her morning runs were one of the few opportunities she had to get out of her own head and just *be*. She couldn't wait to get back to it once Baby Beckett was born. But with the size of her stomach right now, she was well past running anywhere, and for now, brisk walking—which she suspected looked more like a waddle—would have to do.

Working with Slade would likewise *have to do*. The man was infuriating on so many levels. It couldn't possibly be good for her blood pressure to be constantly around him. And even that would be a potential problem. The thought made her chuckle. She could only imagine what would happen if she so much as hinted to the overbearing cowboy that his presence was causing her pulse to rise, putting the baby at risk.

Just kidding.

He'd be racing her to Dr. Delia's faster than she could say *boo*.

After another minute's walk she spotted the stable on the far corner of the block, located across the street from the park. She was getting her bearings around town and even becoming more used to the sounds and smells of country life. She didn't know that she would have intentionally traded the conveniences of city life for Serendipity's slower pace if she'd carefully considered the matter, but she'd made that decision sight-unseen the night she'd married Brody in a spur-of-the-moment Las Vegas wedding.

She would have followed Brody to his childhood home in a second once they were married had Brody given her any encouragement to do so, instead of renting an apartment in Houston as they had. And now that she was carrying his baby, she wasn't about to turn her back on her obligations. The way she saw it, whether she'd come home with Brody back when they'd first married or now, without him and grieving for him, she would have ended up in Serendipity.

It was inevitable. She just wished it hadn't happened in a way that left her feeling so alone.

Baby Beckett picked that moment to jam his or her heel into her rib, a sharp, active and very real reminder that she wasn't alone—and that she had the most important reason of all to make her life in the country work.

Brody's child.

She started toward the interior of the building but her attention was drawn toward a large corral where she saw a gaggle of teenage girls hanging over the side of a split-rail fence, clearly and quite loudly vying for the attention of whomever was inside. Probably some cowboy strutting his stuff for the poor, impressionable teenagers.

Some cowboy. She scoffed and shook her head, playing a hunch as she changed direction and headed for the corral. Slade was such a show off, especially to females. Even—or maybe especially—to the young, impressionable ones. And the old ladies who got a kick out of the handsome cowboy flirting with them. And women of every age in between.

Except for her.

It took Laney a moment to insert herself between two of the giggling girls before she could see who they were cheering for.

Her gaze landed on a single dark-haired cowboy and her smile dropped like lead. Her breath froze in her lungs.

It was Slade, all right. She'd expected as much. What she hadn't been prepared to see was that he was crouched on top of a fearsome-looking bull, shifting his weight and adjusting the strap across his hand, which, as far as Laney could see, was the only thing between him and disaster.

Or death.

What was he thinking?

Had he abandoned all sense? He'd recently lost his

best friend in a bull-riding incident and he was *riding* again?

What kind of fool even did that? He was certifiable. Crazy. Out of his mind.

"Slade," she called, not expecting him to hear her over the chatter of the silly girls who continued to egg him on. The animal snorted and butted at the metal gate and Slade appeared to be completely in the moment, his attention solely on the bull underneath him, but at the last second he lifted his head and his gaze met hers.

Then someone opened the gate and the bull was loose.

Laney couldn't breathe, couldn't move at all beyond tightly gripping the fence, not even caring when splinters pierced the soft skin of her palms. She was certain her heart had stopped beating.

She remembered the first rodeo she'd been to, the one where she'd met Brody. She'd been impressed by the strength and athleticism of the bull riders and had been especially flattered when she'd been approached by one of them. Brody Beckett, with his fair good looks and charming smile, had simply swept her right off her feet.

Time stood still as Lancy watched Slade. This wasn't even a rodeo. It was a guy on a bull in a mostly empty corral with only one cowboy there to spot him. How would he even know when his ride was supposed to be finished?

More to the point, how did a man even stay on such an angry beast, even for one second, never mind eight? Slade made it look easy. With effortless grace and athleticism, he anticipated the bull's every move and brilliantly compensated, even when the animal dug in all four feet and hopped sideways and backward.

After what seemed like forever, a buzzer sounded and the man spotting Slade pulled his horse in close so Slade could jump to safety, if that's what it was. The way Laney saw it, he practically flew off the bull, seriously jarring his body when he landed on his feet and jogged a couple of feet to regain his balance.

Slade bent to retrieve his black Stetson, which he'd lost about halfway through his ride. He raked his fingers through his hair, replaced his hat, and tipped it in her direction. Or maybe he was acknowledging his little fan club. She didn't know and she didn't care.

Laney felt the heat rising to her cheeks as her breath returned to her lungs. Her heart, which had only moments before been a still, solid mass in her throat now jolted back to life and started beating with all the vengeance of a jackhammer.

Slade disappeared behind the high row of bullpens. Laney pulled her hands from the fence and picked at the sharp splinters, welcoming the pain to distract her. Better than thinking about what she was going to do to Slade when she saw him.

"Laney." Slade's rich, deep voice came from over her left shoulder and she stiffened but did not turn. The teenage girls' chattering increased exponentially, sounding as if they'd gone from a few sparrows to an entire flock of geese. Laney watched Slade from the corner of her eye and was surprised when he didn't so much as acknowledge his young fans.

Instead, he moved in right next to Laney, leaning a forearm against the fence and bracing a foot on the lower rail. The long sleeves of his dirty white Western shirt probably prevented him from getting the splinters Laney had received, but it would have served him right if he'd picked up one or two, or a whole log's worth of them.

Feeling as if she were about to boil over, she refused to look at him until he nudged her shoulder with his.

"So, what did you think?"

What did she think? What did she *think*?

She whirled on him and let him feel the full force of her fury. Anger and grief and a surprisingly heavy dose of anxiety coursed through her as she glared daggers at him, clenching her fists as tension rolled through her.

This wasn't about thinking. It was about feeling. And right now she was feeling—well, she didn't even know. Just that he'd opened something in her that she desperately wanted to remain closed.

Unable to contain herself any longer, she reached for his chest and took handfuls of his shirt in her fists. At first she had the notion of shaking some sense into him, but the man was built like a tree. She could have pushed all day and he wouldn't have budged.

Not unless he wanted to.

He wrapped his large hands over hers, completely encompassing them, but instead of forcefully breaking her hold on his shirt, he lightly brushed the rough pads of his thumbs across the backs of her hands.

There was pride striking back from the depths of his blue eyes, but there was confusion, too, and other emotions Laney couldn't put a name to, which made her feel even more vulnerable than she already was.

"How could you?" she choked out. Slade's gentle response had taken the wind from her sails and her voice sounded more like a sob than a demand. "How could you go back to riding bulls after what happened to Brody? Don't you have any sense at all? Any kindness in your heart, knowing that I'd be here—that I'd see? Did you even think about what I might be feeling?"

His features hardened and his brow lowered.

She knew what she was about to say wasn't a fair question, but she couldn't seem to stop herself. Her tongue was lashing out with all the fury of a horse whip, her emotions a runaway train with no brakes to stop her from falling over the edge of the ravine.

"Never mind me—don't you care about Brody at all?"

Chapter Five

Laney's words were a direct hit to Slade's gut. When he had invited her to meet him at the stable, he supposed he had had some backward, mixed up notion that she'd appreciate what he was trying to do. Serendipity's annual rodeo was coming up and he was planning to ride—to honor Brody by competing in the sport that had meant so much to him.

And if he was being completely honest, he might have been trying to show off to her. Just a little bit.

Truthfully, it hadn't even occurred to him how the situation might appear to her. Of course she was furious with him. She probably didn't understand what bull riding was all about. She wouldn't know it had been nothing more dangerous than a practice run and that he'd been riding far below his skill level.

All she'd seen was a man on a bull.

No wonder she was freaking out.

"Laney," he groaned from deep in his throat. He shifted his hands to her shoulders, brushing his palms down her arms to her elbows and then back up again.

"Princess, I'm an idiot. I didn't even think how this would look to you."

She sniffed and made quick work of brushing her cheek with the back of her hand, but he'd seen the tears, and he could feel the tension rippling across her shoulders. He'd really messed up this time. Brody would have been appalled with him not only for inadvertently hurting Laney but for the ever-present possibility of putting the child at risk.

He'd let down his best friend. *Again.*

He was *so* not good at processing emotional stuff, and here he was with the self-charged duty of protecting a pregnant woman with all kinds of wacky hormones raging through her. How much more electric and supercharged could this situation be?

Over Laney's shoulder, Slade saw motion and realized the group of silly teenage girls who'd been watching him were still around, gawking at the two of them and gossiping amongst themselves.

Not cool. One sharp look and a jerk of his head sent the young ladies scurrying for another place to prattle. Probably wouldn't stop the gossip, but he didn't give a fig about that. Folks could say what they wanted. No never mind to him, and hopefully not to Laney, either. She'd been through too much to succumb to wagging tongues.

With the girls gone, he returned his attention to Laney. She couldn't even look him in the eye. She sniffled again, and before he knew what was happening, she wrapped her arms around his waist and buried her face in his chest. She gripped him as if she were afraid if she let go he would disappear, and soon her whole body was quivering. He realized she was sobbing, quietly muffled by the fabric of his shirt.

Whoa. He totally hadn't expected that reaction.

He stood frozen for probably longer than he should have before he wrapped his arms around her and brushed his palm lightly over her back. How was he supposed to deal with a crying female? He felt gangly and awkward, especially with the baby bump between them.

What had happened to the smooth-talking man who knew just how to handle the ladies, what to say to keep them happy? Slade wanted to cheer Laney up, but that part of his character had decided to desert him at the worst possible moment.

"It's going to be all right, princess," he murmured close to her ear.

"It's never going to be all right." She leaned back enough to meet his gaze, though she didn't immediately remove herself from his arms. Her eyes were glassy, but he was relieved to see the spark was back. "And don't call me princess."

Slade took that to mean their moment—or whatever it was—was over. "No offense intended."

She stared up at him for a beat, taking his measure, and then shrugged out of his arms. He wished she'd say something, even if it was to yell at him for his stupidity in bringing her out here, but she didn't say a word. The air thickened between them, ripe with tension.

She was clearly waiting for something.

Like what? For him to beg her forgiveness? Maybe grovel a little bit?

He knew he was at fault, but begging wasn't going to happen. He was too proud to grovel. Still, he supposed an apology of some sort was in order. She deserved that much, at least. Slade knew what Brody would have done at this moment. He would have shoved Slade forward and reminded him what a lug he could be. And he would have made him apologize.

Slade swept his hat off his head and cleared his throat.

"Um—sorry." He didn't even sound like himself. His voice had come out high and squeaky, and he cringed.

Words. Not his forte.

Her gaze widened. "Sorry? That's it? That's all I'm going to get? You scare ten years off my life and that's all you're going to give me? Sorry?"

"What else do you want from me?" The muscles in his shoulders tightened and he fought the temptation to turn and walk away.

Laney had the unique ability to set him on edge. She had when he'd first known her—when she'd first started taking up all of Brody's time and attention—and she did now. The woman couldn't even accept an apology when it was earnestly offered.

"For starters, why don't you try and explain to me what you were doing up on that bull in the first place."

He jammed his hat back on his head and pulled it low over his furrowed brow to shade his eyes both from the glare of the sun and from the glare of the woman beside him.

"I'm a bull rider." He would have thought that part would have been obvious. What did she expect of him?

She frowned. "All guts and glory and absolutely no sense whatsoever. Tell me something I don't know."

Well, at least she thought he had guts.

"Serendipity's annual town rodeo is coming up in

a month and a half. I have every intention of winning the purse." He paused. "For you and for Brody's kid."

"Don't be ridiculous. I don't need your money, and I certainly don't want to be responsible, even indirectly, for you putting yourself at the risk of breaking something just for a few dollars."

"I'm not going to break anything," he assured her, but then he took a mental step backward. His confidence had been shaken after Brody's death. Slade and Brody had both attacked bull riding with the typical arrogance and self-assurance of young men years before. No one could touch them and nothing could hurt them.

But something had. A bull called Night Terror. Brody had been at least as skilled in the arena as Slade was, and it hadn't helped him.

Accidents happened. People died. Good people. The best.

Slade couldn't assure Laney of anything. Not really.

But neither could he *not* follow through with his plan, though he wasn't sure he'd be able to explain his reasoning to Laney. In fact, he was pretty certain he couldn't. It was more a gut feeling of somehow setting things to right rather than anything he could express in words. Only that it was something he needed to do.

"It's to honor Brody's memory."

"I think he'd rather you honor him by staying al— uh—in one piece."

Slade withheld a grimace. He knew he was dredging up all kinds of horrible memories. This might not be the best time to mention that not only was he going to ride in the rodeo, but he hoped beyond hope he would pull Night Terror. He had something to prove.

She cocked a brow and stared at him until he was

certain she was reading every thought in his head. He broke his gaze away from her. There was nothing more unnerving than the thought of a woman in his head, especially Laney. He still wasn't completely convinced she hadn't messed with Brody's heart and mind, confused him and wanted him to change his entire life for her.

No, thank you. That was *not* for him. He'd stay in the shallow end of the relationship pool, even if it felt a little less than satisfying.

And what she didn't know about the rodeo wouldn't hurt her, right?

Because despite all the tussles they had with each other, especially recently, Laney did have one redeeming quality Slade couldn't quite overlook.

She had loved Brody. Despite everything, she'd loved Brody.

And she carried a great deal of strength in her heart. He hadn't known that back then, when he may not have been the best influence on Brody, but he knew it now. Not many women would pack up and move their whole life to a strange town to live with in-laws she barely knew. Wouldn't it have been easier for her to remain with her sister, where Slade had been given to understand she'd been living before she arrived at the Becketts'?

She wasn't taking the easy way out. She wasn't thinking only of herself. She was thinking of her baby—of Brody's baby. Slade had to respect her for that, at least. Nothing she'd gone through in recent months could have been comfortable for her.

He gave her credit, but he still didn't trust her. Once upon a time she'd gotten into Brody's head and turned him all around, trying to change him, to make him into something he was not. Who was to say she wouldn't try the same thing with him? It was a fine line to walk, needing her to trust him and allow him to be part of Baby Beckett's life without giving too much of himself away in the process.

"Is there someplace we can go that's a little more conducive to conversation than standing outside a stable?" She picked at her hand, which was swollen and red from the tiny pieces of wood she must have picked up on the corral fence.

Slade inwardly cringed at the reminder that he'd been the one to bring her here. He'd been the one to thoughtlessly tear open wounds which had barely begun to heal.

"We could grab a coffee at Cup O' Jo's Café," he suggested. "My treat."

It seemed like the least he could do, given the events of the day.

Her gaze met his and she shook her head. "I don't think—"

"I'll even spring for dessert." He couldn't let her finish her statement. Not if it meant she was going to say no to him. He shouldn't be surprised that she wouldn't want to be seen with him in public. She'd probably picked up on those silly teenagers and their giggling. Not good. He didn't know why it was suddenly so important that she accept his offer. Maybe it was just a jab to his ego. He wasn't used to being turned down for a date.

Not a date.

Whatever was the opposite of a date. That's what this was. Frankly, he'd be surprised if the two of them could keep from bickering for the length of time it took them to consume a cup of coffee. They seemed to have developed a process, their way of working things out between each other, and it wasn't anything he'd want to air in public, picking at each other like a couple of bantam hens. He reminded himself to be on his best behavior. He didn't want Laney's dignity, not to mention his own, to take a hit.

Slow. Slightly unsteady. Often uncomfortable. Sometimes painful. That's how it seemed to be between them.

Laney appeared to be reconsidering, or at least she hadn't barked out an immediate rejection. "Well, if you're throwing in chocolate."

He grinned, feeling as if he'd just won, if not the purse, then at least a ride.

"But only because Baby Beckett has a craving."

She was distancing herself from him again, but he'd take what he could get. "Glad to be of service."

Cup O' Jo's was only a block and a half away from the stable. Laney insisted they walk. She had kept herself in very good shape for a seriously pregnant woman. As he recalled, she'd always been slim, with just the right amount of curves. Her baby bump simply added one more. But even if she was in the best shape of her life, Slade wasn't entirely convinced she ought to be straining herself, as far along as she was.

He focused on keeping his own stride short and his pace slow. Their walk was made in an uneasy silence. He didn't want to bring up anything that might send them down the path of a serious conversation, even about the ranching business—not when he knew they'd be interrupted the moment they walked into the café. He didn't want to get into it and then have to drop it— whatever *it* was.

He'd never been good at making small talk. Thankfully, Laney didn't seem to mind the silence, though it hung over Slade like a rain cloud. With his concentrating on keeping their walk to a painfully slow pace, it felt like forever before they reached the café, though it had probably been only a few minutes.

"I'm going to go use the facilities to wash up," he said as they entered Cup O' Jo's. "I smell like cattle."

"Yes. Yes you do," Laney said with a smile, though it didn't quite reach her eyes.

She didn't have to agree with him.

"Shoo, cowboy." Jo Spencer, the vivacious old redhead who owned the café, bobbed up to them and immediately took over the conversation. "Go clean yourself up and I'll seat this pretty lady. Laney, isn't it?"

Laney's gaze widened and Slade interpreted the surprised glance she flashed him as a moment of panic.

Once again he hadn't thought all the way through his actions. He hadn't considered the café scenario any more than he'd worked the bull-riding situation to its logical end. Laney was Brody's widow, and pregnant, to boot. Even though Slade knew his neighbors were the best kind of folks, they were bound to talk about her. If Laney wasn't used to small-town living, then how would she feel when a complete stranger knew her name?

He needed to reassure her that all was well, and so he threw what he hoped looked like a friendly arm over her shoulder and drew her toward him so he could speak to her without being overheard. He was happy for the blaring fifties music and the hum of the crowd that helped drown out his words.

"Don't worry, princess. Jo may come off as a little

domineering, invading your personal space and all, but she's harmless enough. She makes it her business to know everything about everyone. Super nice, though. You won't find a better person in the whole town."

She clearly hadn't anticipated his move and braced her hand on his chest to catch her balance, and then stood on tiptoe so she could whisper back to him.

"Jo's not the domineering one in this scenario." Her eyes were blazing and he realized once again he hadn't given her enough credit. Brody might not even have realized it during his whirlwind romance with the woman, but Laney was as strong as they came. Little minx was a regular spitfire.

He bent his head when she tugged on his shirt, apparently not quite finished with what she had to say.

"And don't call me princess."

Laney guessed from the way the voices of the patrons in the café tapered off and then swelled again that she was the new topic of conversation in the room, but it didn't really bother her. She didn't feel particularly self-conscious, especially after several people, including the cook and his wife, came by her table to introduce themselves. Everyone was so friendly and welcoming.

She didn't know what Slade had been worried about. There was a moment's hesitation when she wondered if the story of Brody's rocky marriage had been tossed about town, but if it had been, she couldn't tell. No one treated her any differently.

She'd seen most, if not all, of these people at Brody's funeral, but she'd been so physically and emotionally ill at that point that most of her memories were a blur. Then she'd left straight afterward for her sister's, and so had never had the opportunity to put names with faces. Now that she would be living here, she was anxious to get to know her neighbors and make new friends.

"Better?" Slade asked as he slid into the vinyl booth opposite her.

"You or me?"

"Well, I meant me and my rodeo dirt, but it's fine if you want to talk about yourself instead." He arched his eyebrows suggestively, and she wondered if the man even knew how to relate to a woman outside of flirting. Or fighting. He leaned his arm across the back of the booth and his biceps flexed with the motion. Was that a practiced move?

"Absolutely not." She didn't even have to think about that answer. "I do not want to talk about me."

She wasn't at all inclined to lead the conversation her direction, except… Her contrary heart wanted answers for the one thing that had been bothering her ever since she and Slade had become reacquainted.

He was silent and watching her intently.

"There is one thing—"

She paused as Jo poured decaf coffee for them and served them each a huge slice of warm peach pie à la mode. Laney tested the coffee against her lips as she considered how to phrase her question. Her curiosity was going to get the best of her, although the truth might be more painful than she imagined. Maybe it was because of her emotional state with her pregnancy and all, but she was seeking some kind of reassurance about her relationship with Brody, that it hadn't all been for nothing. Unfortunately, only Slade could give her that information.

"I'd like to hear about you and Brody." She figured

she'd start there and try to lead the conversation in the direction she desired.

Slade's eyes were an electric blue and sparks were flying. His jaw tightened and his biceps rippled with strain. "What do you want to know?"

What had she said that had put him on the defensive? He looked as if he was ready to come out fighting.

"Other than Grant and Carol, whom I came clean with when I moved to Serendipity, you're the only one who knows the story—the *whole* story."

"What?"

"That Brody and I were separated. That there was a reason we weren't living together as man and wife at the time of his death. But even I don't know the rest of it. Why he never brought me home. Not once. He was keeping me a secret from his family. His friends. The town. And I want to know why."

She'd just told him she didn't want to talk about herself and then she'd plunged right into the deep end, exposing her most personal and vulnerable side.

And to think she intended the original question to be about how Slade and Brody had started riding bulls and how long they'd been doing it. Instead...

"You think he didn't bring you home because he was ashamed of you?" Slade looked and sounded stunned.

"Wasn't he?" She tried to keep the bitterness from her tone but knew she wasn't entirely successful in her endeavor. And she'd completely ruined any chance she had of gently leading the conversation the way she'd intended it to go. She wasn't talking about Brody and Slade at all. She'd already managed to bring it right around to the strained subject of her marriage to Brody, which had very little to do with Slade at all.

"No." Slade leaned forward on his elbows. "Whatever else you might think about Brody, he was in love with you. Always."

"Then, why?"

He raised his eyebrows at the question as if he didn't understand what she was asking.

"You know what I'm talking about. He put me up in an apartment in Houston, like he didn't want anyone to know about me. He didn't even stay with me most of the time. He was either doing police work here in Serendipity or fooling around on the local rodeo circuit."

Slade winced. She'd definitely hit home.

"What did he tell you about where he was?" he asked, his voice husky.

"Not much. Only that he was working toward getting us somewhere permanent to stay before he brought me here. That it was supposed to be a surprise for me. But none of that was true, was it? We both know he already had a home in Serendipity. And he was never going to bring me there."

"He would have." Slade's jaw ticked with strain and he was avoiding her gaze. "He would have."

"You know very well that we were separated," she hissed, trying to keep her voice down and maintain a tenuous hold on her emotions, which were jumping all over the place.

The café was definitely not the place to be having this conversation, and she desperately wished she hadn't opened the can of worms in the first place.

"I was completely on the level when I told you he was coming back to you." Slade threaded his fingers through his thick black hair and rubbed at the knotted muscles of his neck. "I wasn't just telling you what I thought you wanted to hear."

"Why should I believe that?"

"Because it's true." He half stood, and then, after realizing he was drawing the attention of other patrons, regained his seat with a frustrated grunt. "He wanted to reconcile with you, more than anything in this world. And he had every intention of bringing you home to the ranch, I promise you that. He just—he wanted it to be right."

She wanted to believe him. She needed to trust what Slade was saying. Her heart ached for closure.

Baby Beckett moved and she rubbed a hand absently over her ribs. Oh, how she would love to believe that if things had been different, she and Brody and their little baby might have been a real family. If their lives had played out differently.

If Brody hadn't ridden that horrible bull.

Slade stood abruptly, threw a twenty-dollar bill on the table and rubbed his palms down the front of his jeans. "I'm sorry, Laney. You'll never know how sorry I am."

And then he was gone, striding out of the café without a backward glance.

What had just happened?

Whatever it was, Laney knew instinctively it was something significant. For maybe the first time since they'd met, Slade had extended genuine sympathy to her.

And then he'd walked away.

Was she imagining the change in Slade's demeanor? Something didn't feel right or ring true. The man wasn't in the habit of apologizing, for starters, and anyway, what did he have to be sorry for?

"He lit out of here like his tail was on fire." Jo Spencer slid into the spot Slade had vacated and offered Laney a heartfelt smile, kindness and empathy in her gaze. "Putting him in his place, were you?"

Laney started to answer Jo's question but couldn't manage to get a word in edgewise.

"Well, good for you. It's been my experience—and I've had plenty, mind you—that most men need to be knocked down a peg or two now and then, especially the handsome ones like Slade. Their egos tend to swell bigger than their brains. And who better to pop that balloon than us ladies, don't you think?"

Jo cackled and Laney couldn't help but join in the laughter. Not one word the old woman had said was spoken with malice, but rather with affection. The boisterous redhead was probably one of the nicest women she'd ever met. A person couldn't *not* like her.

"Actually, I don't know what that was," Laney said, bemused. "I don't think I'll ever understand that man's mind."

Jo reached across the table and patted her hand. "If I were you, my dear, I wouldn't even try."

That was good advice. Why should she care what Slade thought about anything? He'd been nothing but a thorn in her side since the first day she'd laid eyes on him, strutting around the rodeo with Brody as if the two of them owned the place.

"Are you settling in?" Jo asked in a blatant attempt to change the subject. "Meeting folks from town?"

"A few. I've been so busy with trying to learn the ins and outs of ranching that I haven't had much time for social activities." Nor the inclination, though she wasn't about to tell Jo that. She didn't want to hurt the woman's feelings and wasn't convinced Jo would even understand her reluctance.

"You'll be wanting to make an exception for tonight, dear."

"Why? What's tonight?" Laney felt unaccountably weary, and the last thing she wanted to do was spend more time in public. Regardless, she flashed Jo a polite smile, hoping her expression wouldn't give away the strain she was feeling.

"First Tuesday of the month. Jam session at the community center, six o'clock sharp. It's a Serendipity tradition. You won't want to miss it. You know where the community center is located?"

"I do. But what's a jam session?" It sounded like something a bunch of teenage boys would do in their garages on weekends. "Heavy metal, lots of bass guitars?"

Jo chuckled and waved her arm at Laney. "Maybe in a larger town. Here, the musically talented among us bring their instruments and voices and treat the rest of us to some good old-fashioned country music."

Despite her fatigue, she had to admit that seeing how a small town celebrated and found joy in their everyday lives piqued her interest. And she liked music.

"Trust me, it will be worth your time. You'll come?"

She couldn't deny Jo, not with the anticipation and delight that lit her eyes like firecrackers. She looked as excited as a small child at Christmas.

"I'll do my best to be there."

"Or be square," Jo added with another laugh. She pointed to her tye-died T-shirt, which indeed sported a square, with the words Don't Be printed in the middle of the shape.

Laney glanced at her cell phone for the time. "I'd better hurry if I'm going to have time to go home and change first. What does one wear to a jam session, anyway?" she asked, feeling uncomfortably big-city.

"Calls for formal wear."

A country gathering with formal wear? Great. Laney didn't have a single thing in her pregnancy wardrobe that would even remotely qualify as close to formal, and there was no prospect of fitting into her standard little black dress. That was a possibility that had long passed her.

"*Serendipity* formal wear," Jo added with a gleeful chuckle. "Jeans, dear. Blue jeans and cowboy boots."

Chapter Six

Slade strummed his thumb over the strings of his acoustic guitar and winced at how out of tune it sounded. Adjusting his seat on the stool, he plucked first one string and then another, adjusting each one until he could strum a chord that didn't sound as totally off-key as his insides were feeling.

He wished it was as easy for him to put his life in tune as it was to tune his guitar. There weren't any easy adjustments he could make to solve *those* problems.

Usually the monthly jam sessions raised his spirits, but he doubted even music could reach him tonight. Though he continued to show up to play and sing, he didn't find nearly as much joy in it as he used to.

For one thing, Brody's drum set stood empty at the back of the stage. On occasion one teenager or another would pick up a pair of drumsticks and accompany the band with percussion, but every month since Brody's death they'd left the set empty during Brody's favorite songs as a tribute to him.

It was still hard for Slade to reconcile himself to Brody's death. Sometimes he expected to look up and see Brody pounding out a rhythm, his white-blond hair bobbing to the beat. But even harder was trying to reconcile the wrongs he was only now realizing he was accountable for.

For Brody. For Laney. And even for Baby Beckett.

He was directly responsible for Brody's death. He didn't think he'd ever figure out how to live with that knowledge, but he owned it. And he was just now starting to see what else he had done, things that had hurt people far more than he'd realized. Instead of supporting Brody when he was struggling with the emotional aftermath of his hasty, and some would say reckless, marriage, he'd encouraged his friend to ignore the vows he'd made, and to continue living like a carefree bachelor. He hadn't wanted to share Brody's time and attention with anyone. In some ways he supposed he'd felt as though Laney had taken Brody away from him, and Slade had fought back. If it wasn't for cowboy church, Slade still wouldn't know there was a better way to go through life.

Oh, the irony. Now he *knew* there was a better way, but he had no idea exactly what it was or how to find it. Jesus's death on the cross had reconciled his heart to God. He believed that, but for what purpose? It was all head knowledge, and not even a whole lot of that. He felt like a kindergartner in an algebra class. Without Brody, Slade was walking a lonely, jagged path with no signs to point him in which way to go.

He was too ashamed to go to church. Maybe eventually he'd get his nerve up, but he'd been a reckless teenager who'd turned into an irresponsible man. How could he just show up for church like none of that mattered, as if he belonged in a group with people who had always done the right thing? He'd tried to read his Bible, but without guidance he wasn't getting very far.

He turned his thoughts back to the present as the other musicians, ranging in age from sixteen to seventy, started trickling in, greeting Slade and setting up their equipment. A second acoustic guitar, an electric bass, an ancient piano that was kept in the community center and wheeled out for the jam sessions, and three fiddles. Old Frank Spencer and a couple of other men checked the decrepit sound system to make sure it was working as well as it could be. Slade checked his mic and gave Frank a thumbs up, then glanced up and straight into Laney's beautiful brown eyes.

His heart jumped into his throat. She looked every bit as surprised as he felt. What was she doing here? She hadn't expressed any interest in attending community events.

No, that wasn't quite right. He'd never invited her, had never even thought to mention it to her. Someone else had done the honors.

Add that to his ever-growing list of Never Thought To's where Laney was concerned. Yet another black mark on his record.

He grinned and winked at her, falling back on his usual, most comfortable method of dealing with the fairer sex, especially since his mind was flailing all over the place and he couldn't think of anything else to do.

Only it didn't work with Laney, and it didn't make Slade feel comfortable, either. She rolled her eyes at what Slade belatedly realized she might have interpreted as an openly flirtatious gesture—which was the furthest thing from the truth. Of course he hadn't meant it that way. She should know better. He felt an unfamiliar jolt of embarrassment and heat flooded to his face. Everything about his encounters with Laney were way out of his comfort zone, and this was no exception.

Fortunately for him, she quickly turned her gaze away when Jo Murphy approached her and soon she was deep in conversation with the gregarious redhead. No doubt Jo had been the one to invite her to the community event. Once again Slade chastised himself for the oversight.

Samantha Davenport, the church organist and all around talented keyboardist, slid behind the piano. Taking their cue from her, the others took up their instruments. The drum set sat empty and a blast of pain hit Slade's chest, jarring the breath out of him. It was worse than being thrown from a bull and slamming straight down onto his back in the dirt. Definitely not the condition he wanted to be in when he was supposed to be starting a set of songs.

How could he sing when he couldn't even breathe?

Slade was generally the group's leader and the band was looking to him for the cue to begin. Despite the pain in his chest, he whispered the name of a high-energy country romp and leaned into the mic.

"Glad to see everyone out here tonight."

The crowd quieted and then broke out in applause. He searched for Laney and found her on the outside edge of the room, leaning against a concrete pillar as if for support. And she was completely alone.

"I don't know how many of you have met Laney Beckett," he said, gesturing in her direction. She became instantly alert, her eyes wide and her expression shocked. She jerked her chin, either begging or maybe warning him not to continue, but he was already all-in, and it was for her own good. "She's Brody's—" he paused around the catch in his voice "—widow. I hope you'll all take a moment to make her feel welcome tonight and introduce yourselves if you haven't already."

There. He hadn't been the one to invite her tonight, but he'd just made sure she wouldn't be standing alone the whole time. Now she wouldn't have time to feel lonely or out of place. A sense of satisfaction swept over him.

A group of teenage girls gathered by the front of the stage, mimicking a concert setting. Slade knew he was the big draw for the impressionable youngsters, but that knowledge no longer swelled his ego. Too much had happened, too many bad things. He was finally growing up, maturing beyond the arrogant cowboy who considered seeking women's attention—any female between seven and seventy—the highlight of his day.

He cleared his throat and began the song, singing the first two lines a cappella before Samantha ran her fingers down the keyboard and joined in with some lively chords. The crowd started clapping, a makeshift rhythm that made the lack of percussion even more pronounced. As the guitars and fiddles joined, Slade put everything he had into the performance, singing and playing to soothe the ache in his heart, and maybe to show off—just a little—to Laney. He'd totally blown the bull-riding thing, so he had a lot to make up for.

Surely she'd like the music. She had to.

He played a second song, and then a third, urging the townsfolk to join in singing the familiar tunes. Despite his best efforts to the contrary, his gaze kept finding Laney's, no matter where she was in the room. She'd long since moved away from the pillar and into the center of the celebrating mill of people, all of whom welcomed her warmly.

Another glance and he realized the majority of those to whom she was speaking were men. *Single* men.

His hackles rose and his strumming become more intense. He should have realized the guys in town would see the attractive woman and go in for the kill.

Have some respect, fellas. Laney's not fresh meat.

She was Brody's *widow*, and she was nearly eight months pregnant, for pity's sake. Did these guys have no sense whatsoever? Never mind that, at least in the past, he had been as guilty as the next man for seeing a pretty face and not the person underneath.

But Laney? This was too much.

"Set's over," he announced when the song ended.

"But we've only done four songs," Samantha protested, backed by the whole slew of muttering musicians.

"Fine. Then play without me." He pulled the guitar strap over his head and set the instrument on a nearby stand.

Samantha shook her head, clearly flummoxed at his behavior, but directed the band into another song—a ballad. Folks started pairing off for impromptu dancing and Slade increased his pace, determined to break through the thick crowd before some idiot asked Laney to dance. He could only imagine what kind of angst that would leave her with.

He caught up with her just as one of the men in her circle of admirers leaned down to whisper something in her ear. Seth Howell, recently back in town from his army deployment, was already being way too familiar with Laney. His hand brushed across her shoulders as he bent his head to hear her response.

Her *laughter*.

Slade couldn't understand why she would be encouraging the soldier. His pulse hammered and his gaze clouded with anger and resentment as she smiled up at Seth and blinked those amazing brown eyes of hers.

He couldn't believe what he was seeing—Laney with her rounded belly, flirting like there was no tomorrow. What had this world come to?

He overheard Seth using the word *dance* and watched as he gestured toward an open spot close to the front of the stage, and it was all Slade could do to keep his cool and not deck the man for his impertinence. Slade wasn't used to *experiencing* such strong emotions, much less containing them.

He didn't pause to consider why that was. He simply reacted. He'd come up on Laney from behind, so she didn't even know he was there until he took her by the shoulders and spun her around and into his arms.

"Sorry, pal. She's with me," he told the soldier, who immediately threw his hands in the air to demonstrate his surrender. Slade couldn't help the smug grin that lined his face when the man backed off.

"Wipe that smile off your face," Laney snapped, glaring up at him. "What do you think you're doing?"

He would have thought it was obvious. Saving her from herself.

Again.

She never got him, did she? Instead, she always assumed the worst about him. Shoot first, talk later.

"I'd think it would be obvious, princess. I'm keeping you from having to say no to that fellow."

"What makes you think I was going to say no?"

He froze midstep and held her at arm's length. "Weren't you?"

One corner of her full lips twitched upward and her eyes glittered with unspoken amusement.

"Very funny." He tightened his grip on her and whirled her around, ignoring the way his senses were reacting to holding her in his arms. His large hands spanned the back of her waist, her lip gloss sparkled from the glow of the overhead lights and the clean, woodsy scent of her perfume wound around and through him.

But this wasn't just any pretty woman. This was *Brody's* Laney, and he had to get his mind elsewhere. *Now.* He was every bit as bad as the other single fellows if he couldn't keep his mind on what really mattered here.

He spun her around, and then again. He wasn't an expert dancer by any means, but he had a pretty good handle on the Texas two-step. He just needed to concentrate on where his feet were going and not on the woman in his arms.

"Why do you feel the constant need to butt into my business?"

Her demand made him feel as if she'd thrown a bucket of ice water over him. Thankfully, the music was so loud it nearly drowned out the question even to his ears. He was fairly certain their conversation wasn't being overheard by the friends and neighbors dancing around him. How humiliating would that be—not only being taken down a notch, but having it done right there in public?

"I don't know." He frowned and tried to shrug it off.

Why did she have to be so serious all the time? "Why do you think?"

"You seriously don't want me to answer that question," she said, playfully swatting his chest.

He let out his breath. So this wasn't a challenge, after all. She was goofing around with him. He didn't know whether to be relieved or alarmed by the knowledge.

"But cut it out," she continued, her gaze narrowing on him. "I don't need you to fight my battles for me. I'm perfectly capable of taking care of myself—and Baby Beckett, if that's what you are worried about."

"Brody would have my hide if I didn't look out for you."

"That's very sweet," she said in a saccharine voice that suggested sarcasm. "But entirely unnecessary, I assure you."

"Fine." He didn't see a point in arguing with her. They'd been over this territory many times before, and revisiting the matter wouldn't change anything. He was still going to watch out for her and protect her—from outside forces, and from herself, when necessary—and she would no doubt continue complaining about it.

"Great music," she said. Slade was relieved at the abrupt change in subject. Finally, she was giving him a break. "I'll admit I was a little skeptical when Jo first told me about the *jam session*."

He chuckled. "Why? What did you expect?"

"I don't know. Heavy metal played by a bunch of high school kids?"

His chuckle turned into an all-out laugh. "In Serendipity? Princess, this is cowboy country."

Her eyes narrowed on him in an unspoken warning. What? What had he said?

"Exactly," she said after a moment's hesitation. "I'd call this a—a hoedown, maybe. A country dance."

He winked at her. "We have those, too. Square dancing. Line dancing. A little more organized than anything you'll be seeing tonight. This is more casual. It's also open-mic, if you're interested in joining in the singing."

She shook her head. "That is *so* not going to happen. God gifted you with a wonderful voice, but me? Not so much."

"I'm sure you're exaggerating."

"No, I'm really not. But you—you've got a beautiful voice."

"I'm not sure I like my voice being called beautiful." He grinned down at her. "Sounds kind of lame."

"Feminine, you mean? You are such a *guy*." She made it sound like an insult. "It sounds even odder to call your voice handsome." She laughed.

He liked hearing her laugh. She was under a tremendous amount of stress between Brody's death, her pregnancy, and now taking on the responsibility of the Becketts' ranch. But tonight she seemed as if a load had been taken off her shoulders.

"I didn't know you played guitar, either."

"Does that surprise you?"

"Yes." She shook her head. "No. I guess it shouldn't, really. We weren't exactly friends after I married Brody."

"No. We weren't." His voice sounded terse and he cleared his throat.

"I just never pictured you performing on a stage, singing and playing acoustic guitar as if you did it for a living. Big, tough bull rider such as yourself?"

"I guess this wouldn't be the time to tell you I've had classical music training."

"No way." She laughed, but he could see the doubt in her eyes and he knew he had her. He grinned like a cat.

"Naw. I'm pulling your leg. I've never had a lesson in my life. Taught myself. I play by ear."

"Okay, you got me," she admitted, chuckling. "I'm even more impressed. That's not easy to do. You continue to surprise me at every turn."

"Is that a bad thing?"

She shook her head, and then changed her mind and nodded. "Sometimes it is. Sometimes not."

"Good. Someone's got to keep you on your toes."

"Is that what you're trying to do?"

He arched his eyebrows and flashed what he hoped was a mysterious look. "Maybe. You'll never know."

"Hmm." She stared up at him for a moment more, and then leaned her cheek against his shoulder. For a moment that was enough, that he and Laney *were*.

Just *were*.

"I noticed the drum set up there on the stage," she said.

Slade wondered if she'd been uncomfortable with the silence between them. He hadn't been. And he didn't really want to go where the conversation had led them.

"Is the drummer sick tonight?"

Every sliver of contentment he'd been feeling instantly vanished, shredded by the truth Slade would rather forget. He leaned away from her so he could meet her gaze.

"Not sick, Laney. Gone."

* * *

The pain in Slade's eyes said it all, even before he'd voiced the words aloud.

Brody.

The drum set was empty because Brody had been the drummer. How had she been married to him for six months and not known that about him? What else was there? What had she missed?

She stumbled. If Slade hadn't had his strong arms wrapped securely around her, she would have fallen into an undignified heap. As it was, he gently led her to a relatively quiet corner of the room without missing a beat of the dance.

"You okay? You look as white as a sheet."

"I just—I didn't know."

"I'm sorry. I should have mentioned it before. That was totally thoughtless of me to drop that on you the way I did."

"It's not your fault. I asked you, and you answered. It's just that—"

Her sentence dropped off as pain and guilt and anger ripped through her, stealing her breath and the beat of her heart.

"Laney." Slade cupped her face in his hands, brushing his thumbs along her cheekbones as his gaze captured hers. "Laney. Look at me, princess. You've got to breathe. Come on, with me now. Breathe in, breathe out."

Laney felt as if she were seeing Slade from a distance, her vision tunneling until she thought she might slip into darkness, but his gaze wouldn't let her go there.

"Don't pass out on me, sweetheart. I know I tend to have that effect on women, but Jo Spencer will have my

hide if you go and faint in my arms, you being pregnant and all."

Laney was beginning to feel nothing could reach her,
but Slade's joke, followed by his deep rumble of laughter, snapped her out of the thick shadows. Air filled her
lungs as if she'd just broken through the water's surface
after almost drowning. She gasped.

Slade sagged in relief and pushed out a breath. Only
then did she see the tension rippling from his neck into
his shoulders and biceps. Odd that she hadn't felt it in
his hands.

"Good thing for you I'm not the fainting type." She
straightened and Slade dropped his arms, shoving them
into the front pockets of his worn blue jeans.

"Brody and I used to dream about being rock stars."
He leaned his shoulder against the nearby wall, giving
her a little bit more breathing space. "I think most kids
do at one point or another. The whole 'jam session in
the garage' really wasn't that far off. We spent many
happy nights playing in our band and dreaming of fame
and fortune."

"I didn't know that about him, that he was a drummer. I imagine there are—" Her lips quivered and she
swallowed hard but couldn't release the lump of emotion
in her throat. "Many things I didn't know about Brody."

Slade frowned, but it was neither condescension nor
censure. Sadness, definitely, and pity, maybe.

"You didn't have the chance. God took him before
you two could ever really get to know each other. That
and—"

He paused as the music ended. Samantha waved at
Slade, gesturing for him to return to the stage.

"Looks like you're up." Laney was actually quite

relieved by the interruption. She didn't want to talk about all the mistakes she'd made in her relationship with Brody.

Mistakes *she'd* made. Up until this moment she'd cast all the blame elsewhere. For as long as she'd known him she'd harbored resentment against Slade for leading her husband astray, and there was some truth in that. But Brody was his own man, and ultimately the decisions he'd made, which had damaged their relationship perhaps beyond repair, had been his to make. Slade might have influenced him, but at the end of the day, Brody was responsible for his own actions.

As she was for hers.

She'd been so busy casting blame elsewhere that she hadn't seen her part in it at all. She'd been so angry when she'd discovered the kinds of things Brody had been doing in his spare time, most of which he'd spent at Slade's side, that she'd swiftly booted him to the curb without even trying to work things out. She'd thought he was riding bulls—not drinking and flirting with women. And when she'd found out otherwise, she hadn't handled it as well as she might have.

It wasn't that she completely blamed herself for what had transpired, but neither could she assign all the responsibility to Brody—or to Slade. There were things she could have done better, things they all could have done better. And who knows that her life might have turned out differently if she'd made other—better—choices.

But it hadn't. All of those actions and decisions had come together to form what had happened. And she couldn't go back—only forward.

She shook her head to dislodge the melancholy thoughts

and turned her attention back to Slade. She'd assumed he was returning to the stage and his guitar, but instead she discovered him running around with a pack of preschool-aged children. He carried one little redheaded girl in his arms, and the child clearly adored him. Apparently he was as equally able to charm the very young ladies as well as the older ones.

He whooped and laughed as he chased a little tow-headed boy who was running through the crowd trying to avoid Slade's touch. Slade appeared almost as youthful and innocent as the children he was playing with. He gave the boy a good chase but let the child get away from him several times before finally tapping the top of the boy's head.

"Tag. You're it!"

Laney's jaw dropped in surprise. The Slade she thought she knew was far too wrapped up in himself to bother with children. She couldn't even imagine him with kids—which was part of the reason she was so hesitant about Slade being a significant part of Baby Beckett's life.

And yet there it was, right in front of her.

Slade smiling and laughing and zigzagging around other adults, trying to avoid the boy's touch. He put up a good show but Laney could see he was purposefully putting himself out there so the boy could tag him.

"Tag. You're it!" the boy exclaimed, proud to have caught up with Slade.

Slade touched him back. "No, you're it."

"No, you're it."

"You got me, scamp." Still holding the little girl in one arm, Slade scooped the boy off his feet and swung him around in a circle. He was definitely having every bit as much fun as the children. Before today, Laney would have chalked it up to his immaturity. But now?

Maybe she was seeing the full-grown man Slade really was.

And she liked it.

Chapter Seven

Slade couldn't wait to see Laney again—because she needed help with the ranch, not because he wanted to see her pretty face. Well, okay, he had to admit he missed her smile, enough that he rushed over directly after work. He didn't even bother taking the time to change out of his police uniform before heading over to the Becketts'.

It had been a really long week and Slade had been putting in plenty of overtime at the station training a couple of new recruits. Serendipity wasn't exactly crime central. They rarely had break-ins and hadn't had a murder—ever. But drug runners occasionally used a route skimming close to their town. And then there was the paperwork—mounds and mounds of the stuff. Teaching young men who'd rather be out saving the world how to sit behind a desk buried in bureaucracy was more difficult than anything else he did.

He found Laney behind the desk in the Becketts' office with her black reading glasses perched on her nose as she ran figures through an adding machine. She looked cute in glasses. They gave her a certain kind of style, and made her amazing eyes appear even larger than they were.

As soon as he entered, she looked up and sighed dramatically, smoothing her hair with her palms.

"Rescue me," she begged him, twisting side to side in her chair to stretch her back muscles. "I have been crunching numbers all day and at the moment I feel like I'm drowning in them."

He chuckled. "Not much of a math person?"

"I can hold my own. But eight hours of staring at columns upon columns of numbers would put a knot in anyone's back."

"I hear you. I've been training rookies all day. Doing paperwork, not shooting a gun." Instinctively his hand hovered over the holster on his belt and Laney's gaze followed the movement.

Her brow furrowed.

"Why the frown?"

She turned her head away, refusing to look at him.

"What? I've been around you long enough to know when you get into a tizzy about something, princess. What did I do now?"

That seemed to do the trick. She met his gaze, her eyes crackling with fire. "I'm not in a tizzy. And don't call me princess."

He raised a brow, daring her to continue to deny that she was in a pique. Something had gotten up the woman's craw, and given their history, he was fairly certain it had something to do with him.

"I just don't like guns," she finally admitted.

"I'm a cop. Guns kind of come with the territory."

He wasn't telling her anything she didn't already

know. Brody had been a member of Serendipity's police force, as well. She'd had experience with men with guns.

"Surely Brody brought his SIG Sauer home with him."

"He knew I didn't like having a gun in the house, so he never let me see it. It went straight into the lockbox the second he walked in the door."

Slade slumped into the chair across the desk from Laney, laced his fingers behind his neck, leaned back and propped his feet on the hard oak surface. She stared at his boots a moment and he waited for her to explode on him for his lack of manners. At least that would get her mind off of the gun. He made a mental note not to come visiting in his uniform anymore. Not a good thing to upset a pregnant woman.

To his surprise, she didn't burst out nagging like he'd thought she would. Instead, she steepled her fingers and rested her chin on them.

"I can guess why you became a cop," she stated bluntly. "And Brody, too, for that matter."

"Yeah? And why is that?" This he had to hear— because from the tone of her voice it sounded as if she were accusing him of choosing to be a career criminal and not the man who caught the bad guys.

"You want to be a hero."

Slade burst out laughing. Whatever he'd expected her to say, that was not it.

"And why would you think that?"

"This town has Wild West stamped all over it. I can totally imagine you riding in on your horse, guns blazing, shooting up the air while your presence alone chases the bad guys out of town. You wear the wrong color of cowboy hat, but other than that, you're a dead ringer for sheriff."

"Somebody has been watching too many old Westerns on television. What's wrong? Are you having problems sleeping at night? Baby keeping you awake?" He grinned at her.

"Read them, actually."

"Right. Your romance novels. Is that how those cowboys do it? Shooting it up through the town?"

"Absolutely. I've always wondered, though, where the bullets go that they shoot into the air."

"Back down again, I would imagine. Gravity and all that." He chuckled at her question, which, now that he thought about it, had some merit.

She laughed. He liked the way it lit up her face, erasing the tension that usually resided there. "You never see that part in the movies, though, do you?"

"Bullets taking out random innocents? I'm guessing it doesn't make for good pleasure viewing."

"Funny, the parts you don't see."

The revelation struck him deep in the chest. She wasn't seeing him. Not really. She was so stuck on what he was wearing—whether as a bull rider or as a cop—that she couldn't look past it. As if the clothes made the man.

He hadn't changed just because he was wearing the uniform, yet her response to him certainly had. What was up with that? Did she know so little about him that the idea of him carrying a weapon disconcerted her? Didn't she trust him at all?

"I could teach you how to shoot." He couldn't begin to guess where that idea had come from, but it sounded like a bad idea as soon as it came out of his mouth. If she didn't like guns, she certainly wouldn't want to learn how to shoot one.

"Now?" She sounded surprised, but also curious.

"Sure. Why not? We've got a couple of good hours of daylight left. I'm sure we can rustle up a few empty aluminum cans.

"Right." She didn't sound too sure of herself, but there was grit and determination in her gaze. A man couldn't help but admire her for that. "Um—okay. If you're game for it, I guess I am, too."

A half an hour later, Slade was propping aluminum cans on the mounded crest of a hill. Laney had said next to nothing since she'd made the decision to learn how to shoot. Only when they'd asked Carol for some cans and she'd given Laney a glowing report of her own experiences shooting did she smile a little, and only for a second.

At the moment, she looked entirely too serious. He fervently wished he had never opened his big mouth in the first place. She was obviously uncomfortable with the idea, and he had the notion she was only going through with it because she felt challenged to do so.

With the soda pop cans set on the small ridge, Slade moved back to where he'd left Laney standing and set her up with safety glasses and earplugs. Even out here on the range the sound of a gun was deafening, especially to someone who wasn't used to it. He removed the clip from his SIG Sauer and checked it, then clicked it back in place in a single smooth movement.

"How do we do this?" she asked. "Standing? Kneeling? I can't go flat on my stomach like I've seen military guys do in the movies."

Slade chuckled despite the tension he was feeling.

No, she definitely couldn't lie on her bulging belly. He had a pretty good notion Baby Beckett would object to that.

"Let's try standing. The handgun has a bit of a kick to it, but I don't think it will be too bad for you."

Or would it? Was it safe for a pregnant woman to fire a gun? If he accidentally put Laney or Baby Beckett in jeopardy with this stupid idea he was going to shoot *himself.*

He started to hand her the gun but she shook her head and laid a hand on his forearm, her eyes wide and glassy.

"Show me."

He nodded. Of course. Some teacher he was, ready to throw a gun into her hands without having demonstrated his technique and the fine points of shooting. He was more convinced than ever that he'd made a mistake in coming here. But there was no way to back down now.

Holding the gun steady in the V of his right hand, he set his stance, his legs braced and his hips at an angle from the target. He pulled the slide back to load a round, cupped his other hand around the bottom of the SIG and took aim down the sight. With the confidence of many hours of practice and training, he lightly swept his index finger over the trigger.

An aluminum can popped and jumped and Laney cheered and applauded.

"Remarkable." For once she actually *looked* impressed, which bumped his ego up a notch or two.

"Remember, I've been doing this a long time. Since I was a boy."

"In other words, you make it look easy when it's

not. I get it. I already know I'm never going to hit a can. Let's just hope I don't accidentally wound a poor, helpless animal out there somewhere."

He chuckled at the dismayed expression on her face. "You don't have much to fear there. That first shot probably scared off any nearby wildlife."

She laughed with him, but it sounded strained. "Well, I'm thankful for that."

"I promise you—by the time we're finished today, you'll have hit one of those cans. I'm teaching you, after all. Trust me and all will be well, princess."

She arched an eyebrow and tipped her chin, not speaking and yet saying volumes.

He flashed a cheeky grin.

"I know. I know. Don't call you princess."

The man was exasperating. Truly and completely exasperating. Mr. Thrill-Seeker, Bull Rider and Adrenaline Junky with his princess this and princess that. And the worst part was, she didn't really mind the silly nickname anymore.

She must be getting weak in the head. Or maybe the knees, but that was just because she'd never shot a gun before. She was fairly certain she couldn't hit the broadside of a barn, much less one of those tiny aluminum cans sparkling in the sunlight.

She'd never backed down from a challenge in her life and she wasn't about to start now, but who knew there were so many things to remember when she was shooting? It wasn't exactly point and click, no matter how easy Slade made it look.

Slade handed the gun to her and helped her adjust her grip. She lifted it toward the target but didn't put her finger anywhere near the trigger. As much as Slade got on her nerves, she didn't want to accidentally shoot him.

"Take a deep breath and relax. You should always treat a gun like it's loaded, even if you're sure it's not."

"Yes, but I *know* it is loaded. I watched you put the clip in."

"Exactly, which is why you're pointing it at the target and not at me," he said with a wink.

She chuckled, but it was a shaky sound.

"—Now, the first thing you need to do is load a bullet in the chamber."

She mimicked what she'd seen him do with the slide and was rewarded with a satisfying click. Her pulse was hammering and exhilaration coursed through her, but it wasn't necessarily a bad feeling.

"That's it. Good. Now sight the can and when you're ready, take a deep breath and brush your finger over the trigger. It's sensitive, so be careful not to press on it too hard. It needs just the slightest touch to fire."

Adrenaline was making her shake so hard that she couldn't keep the gun from quivering no matter how hard she held it in her grasp. She took aim down the sights as best she could, then squeezed her eyes shut and swept her finger over the trigger.

The kick of the SIG sent her reeling backward, right into Slade's arms. Slade hadn't so much as budged when he'd fired the gun. She hadn't seen any evidence of kickback with him, so she didn't expect it to have quite that much force.

Slade took the gun from her, removed the clip and holstered it, all without letting her out of his arms. She'd never seen him look so concerned, or so serious. About anything.

"Are you okay?" he asked, turning her around in his arms. "Is Baby Beckett okay? Are you hurt? I'm so sorry. I never should have suggested this whole thing in the first place. I knew it was a bad idea. I should have stopped it before it started."

"Whoa. Whoa. Whoa." She laid a hand on his chest to halt his avalanche of words. "I'm fine. Really."

"You're not hurt?" He repeated, not looking the least bit convinced. His gaze dropped to her rounded belly. "The baby's okay?"

"Baby Beckett is fine. And give me a little credit, here. I'd never put my child in danger, and besides, I'm tougher than you think. I'm not going to let one small, unanticipated shove from a handgun keep me from new experiences. The truth is, I kind of enjoyed it. Now tell me what I did wrong and let's try this again."

"I don't think—"

"Slade." She didn't let him finish. "Are you going to show me how to shoot this weapon or am I going to have to figure it out all by myself? Because one way or another, it is going to happen. One of those aluminum cans is going to discover its number is up."

He chuckled at her joke but didn't look convinced. He regarded her carefully for a moment, indecision rampant in his expression. Furrowed brow, pressed lips, uncertainty in his gaze.

It seemed like decades before he gave in and shrugged his acceptance of the gauntlet she'd thrown down.

"You closed your eyes."

"What?"

"Your eyes. Just before you pulled the trigger, you squeezed your eyes shut and the barrel of the gun rose."

He unholstered the gun, replaced the clip and gave it back to her.

"Oh." Well, that was deflating. Clearly a rookie move. She hadn't been watching Slade's face when he shot the gun, she'd been watching his stance. His arms. The gun.

She didn't know why she wanted to impress Slade with her shooting skills, but she did. Which meant she had to keep practicing until she got it right. Simple as that—or maybe not so much. "Okay. What else?"

"You might be able to better absorb the kick if we adjust your stance a little bit." He reached for her waist—or where her waist used to be—and gently turned her hips to the angle he'd used when he was shooting.

"You'd think I'd be used to absorbing kicks by now. I'm convinced Baby Beckett is a future soccer player."

He shared a rich, low laugh with her and his chest rumbled against her shoulders. She glanced back at him and grinned.

He cleared his throat. "Okay, then. Back to work. There. Now put a bullet in the chamber and straighten your arms."

He stood directly behind her with his arms on either side of her as he made small adjustments to her shoulders and elbows. She knew she needed to be concentrating on everything he was telling her—she was trying to shoot a *gun*, after all—but all she could think about was the strength of his biceps, the leathery, earthy smell that was distinctly Slade. His warm breath brushed her cheek as he instructed her in the fine points of her grip.

There were a thousand reasons why she shouldn't be thinking about Slade, or feeling the gentle poke of tentative emotions springing up like flowers pushing their way through the uncooperative ground of winter. No matter how many times she inwardly scolded herself for recognizing the chemistry between them, her contrary heart and mind refused to listen.

She knew the exact moment Slade felt it, too. He stiffened but didn't immediately draw away from her. The tension was almost palpably crackling between them and she barely resisted the urge to melt further into his embrace.

Was he struggling as much as she was with what should not and could not be? She should be strong, be the one to break the embrace, or at least shoot the gun. That was bound to break the electric moment between them. But no matter how much her mind told her to withdraw, she could not find the strength of will even to pull the trigger.

Slade made a sound from deep in his throat and stepped away from her. She could see the tension rippling across his shoulders and the tautness around his jaw. Jagged pangs of guilt assaulted her. She felt as if she was betraying Brody—because she missed the sheltered feeling of Slade's embrace the moment it was gone.

Where had this come from?

She barely even *liked* Slade. It didn't make any sense that she would be attracted to him, even remotely. She must be more hormonal than she realized. It was the only explanation that made any sense, and she clung to it desperately.

Slade appeared to be every bit as uncomfortable as she felt. Color rose in his cheeks, staining right through the shadow of stubble on his face. His eyes, always an extraordinary shade of blue, glittered darkly and even more fiercely than usual.

What was he thinking?

She met his gaze for a second but his eyes were unreadable. Had she imagined what had just happened between them? Had she been the only one to feel the chemistry between them? That would be even worse than if he'd felt an attraction as well, because that left her feeling like every kind of fool.

"I think you've got it," Slade said, his usually rich baritone taking on a deeper, huskier quality. "You can shoot whenever you're ready."

He kept a light fingerhold underneath her elbow as a silent reminder to keep her arms steady, but otherwise he physically distanced himself from her and she felt it wholeheartedly, the emptiness where once there was warmth. She hadn't realized until this moment how completely alone she felt.

She'd experienced similar emotions in her life, the barren ache in her chest, only a few times before, as she grieved when her parents had died, and when Brody had been taken from her before his time.

But Slade was here. He was real. Strong. Steady. Alive.

His fingertips barely brushed her elbow and yet every one of her nerve endings was hypersensitive to his touch.

And he was waiting for her to pull the trigger.

Eyes open, she reminded herself silently.

Eyes open.

Her throat was ragged and dry. That was good advice, and not just for shooting the handgun. She needed to keep her wits about her where Slade was concerned.

He was a man with a trail of broken hearts paved miles behind him. She would have to be emotionally blind to entertain the notion of becoming the next in his string of conquests, even for a moment.

That would never happen. She wouldn't *let* it happen. She not only had herself to consider—there was her unborn child. And that reality would affect every decision she made from here on out for the rest of her life.

She took aim, braced for impact and brushed her finger across the trigger. This time she was ready for the pop and kick of the weapon, but not the ting of the bullet hitting aluminum as one of the cans leaped and plunged.

Her breath came out in an audible gasp. Slade whooped and held his hands in the air in the symbol of victory.

"You did it! Only your second time around and you hit the target. That's no easy feat. Way to go, princess."

She wasn't sure whether his enthusiasm stemmed from the fact that she'd hit the can or because he'd been the one to teach her, but she couldn't avoid the pride that welled in her at her accomplishment. She'd hit the target. Who would have thought she had it in her?

She'd done it. Not just shot a gun, but conquered a fear.

And maybe she'd even grown to understand a little more what made men like Brody and Slade tick. She had to admit the flush of adrenaline coursing through her was rather addictive. She felt more alive than she had in months. Was this why men like Slade and Brody did what they did—rode bulls, became policemen, carried weapons?

"You want to give it another go?" Slade asked, his voice laced with enthusiasm. "I still have plenty of rounds left."

Laney shook her head and carefully offered him the gun. She'd wanted to prove something to herself—and maybe to Slade—and she had. But now that she was coming down from the thrill of the moment, her hands were shaking again and her heart was hammering. She thought it was probably best to take a break and rest. She lowered herself onto the blanket Slade had thoughtfully brought along and spread across the grass for her.

She watched as he unholstered his belt and placed the gun in the lockbox he'd brought along with him. He dropped down beside her and stretched his legs, bracing himself on one elbow.

"I knew you could do it." He smiled at her, his gaze warm, and she had to look away in order not to drown in the blue of his eyes.

"I didn't," she admitted softly.

He ran his index finger lightly across her jaw. She forced herself to breathe and not to stiffen under his touch, no matter how much it affected her. She knew better than to give a man like Slade even the smallest hint of acknowledgment, or he would push his advantage, and she wasn't certain she was strong enough to resist it right now.

"You don't give yourself enough credit."

She sputtered. "As I recall, it wasn't all that long ago that you weren't giving me any credit at all."

He had the good grace to wince. "Touché."

"But then again, I didn't give you much of a chance, either, did I?"

"With good reason."

She didn't know what he meant by that statement, but she had the strangest notion they were speaking of completely different things.

"Well, that's all behind us now, isn't it?"

"Is it?"

Now she *knew* he was talking about something different, but what she didn't know was how to ask him what he meant.

"For Baby Beckett's sake," she clarified, hoping he'd take the lead and expand on the subject, give her a hint as to where his mind had gone.

He didn't. He simply shifted his gaze to somewhere over her shoulder and nodded in agreement. "For the baby."

Feeling the conversation was at an impasse, she searched her mind for another less uncomfortable topic.

"Why did you decide to become a police officer?"

"I'm hungry. Are you hungry? I wish I'd thought to pack lunch for us. I could really go for an apple right now."

She raised a brow. He was going to avoid this subject, as well?

He correctly interpreted her expression and shrugged his free shoulder. "I'd like to claim altruism and say it was entirely for the good of the community, but that wouldn't be the truth, or at least the whole truth."

"Why, then?"

"Excitement. The thrill of the moment. The chance to carry a gun. Kind of a tough-guy thing to do. My two older brothers run the ranch my folks passed down to us, so I'm really not needed there. Maybe it would have been different if I'd been like Brody—"

His sentence slammed to a halt, but she didn't interrupt as he gathered his thoughts.

"An only child, that is," he finally continued, his voice gravelly and full of pain. His brow furrowed.

"Grant and Carol both assumed he'd eventually tone down his wild ways and settle on the ranch. And he probably would have, if it hadn't been for me."

She reached for his hand before she had the chance to think better of it. "His legacy will be honored. I promise you that."

"I know."

His gaze met hers. It was the first time since she'd met him that he had affirmed her commitment to doing what was best for Baby Beckett, the first time he'd really acknowledged the reality of her relationship with Brody at all.

"He'd be proud of you, you know." Slade absently linked his fingers with hers. "He would have waved his hat in the air and bragged long and loud about how he'd married the prettiest, bravest woman in all the world. And one who knew how to shoot a gun." His eyes were still sad but one side of his mouth kicked up.

Despite the grief that rose to the surface as they spoke of Brody, she smiled gently. The way Slade had described the scene—that was all Brody. Slade had known and loved his friend in a way she'd never been able to. She'd never been Brody's friend. Had never known him that deeply. She'd never been much of anything to him.

"Did Brody not want to become a rancher?" she asked, realizing that he must have had similar motives for becoming a cop and not settling down at home.

"He wasn't like me. He always wanted to be a part of his family's legacy eventually. He dreamed of the day he'd have a family to share it with—of bringing you home to the ranch, once he fell in love with you." His voice sounded strangled. "The truth is, he followed me on to the police force because I always prodded him to do so. I was a bad influence on him. I knew it, and I let it happen anyway. I was an arrogant jerk."

"I don't see how becoming a policeman would be having a bad influence on him," she said, and realized she meant it. Up until now she'd seen the two only as men pursuing danger on a lark, but now she suspected there was much more to it than that, even if Slade was unwilling to admit it.

His gaze widened. "Being a cop wasn't what he wanted to do with his life. I shouldn't have pushed him to it. And there—there were other ways I led him astray." He gestured toward her with his chin. "Ways that hurt innocent people."

She didn't pretend not to know what he meant. He was honestly acknowledging his part in the way Brody had behaved after their hasty and ill-thought-out marriage. But there was so much more to it than what he was saying aloud, layers she'd only just begun to explore. She wasn't anywhere near ready to discuss it all, to shred through the surface with Slade. And she was fairly certain he didn't want to go there, either.

"Have you ever had to shoot someone?" This time she was the one to throw a question right out of left field, but it had the desired effect. He sat up abruptly and dropped her hand as if it burned him.

"No, I—" He paused. "No, I haven't. And I hope it never comes to that. But I wouldn't hesitate to do so if it was necessary to protect Serendipity, to keep the people I know and love safe from harm."

A week ago, she would not have believed that answer coming from Slade McKenna's mouth. She'd not thought him capable of deep commitment to an honorable cause, much less his ability to admit it out loud.

Yet now, at this moment, she'd not only expected the answer he'd given, but she believed it. It unnerved her to think about the ramifications of what she'd discovered today. Because the Slade she'd built up in her mind as the worst kind of scoundrel was no longer that man.

Maybe he never had been.

Chapter Eight

Slade was anxious to get to the Becketts so he could see Laney again, even if only to test his new theories about her—he hesitated to call them feelings.

Somewhere along the way, something had shifted between the two of them and Slade was at a loss as to how to describe where things stood. He only wished he knew what had changed. He couldn't believe he was admitting this, even to himself, but maybe he'd been unfair in his judgment of Laney. Could his perception of her as a purely selfish woman who'd married Brody and then tried to change him have been so far off?

It was as if his eyes were suddenly opened and he was seeing her for the first time. He'd always acknowledged her outer beauty, even from the first time he and Brody had noticed her. A man would have to be blind not to recognize how pretty she was with her caramel-brown hair and deep chocolate-brown eyes. He'd always assumed that was what Brody had been attracted to—her outward beauty. No doubt that had been part of it. Laney had turned Brody's head from the very first moment he'd met the gorgeous rodeo princess.

But now Slade wondered if that was all it had been. Had Brody recognized what a treasure he had in Laney? That her sweetness extended beyond her appearance and into her heart?

Great. Now he was spouting nonsense, even if it was only in his mind. Next thing he knew, the same drivel would start coming out of his mouth. He'd have to watch everything he said from now on.

And what did it matter, anyway? No matter how Slade's feelings might have started to change, the fact was that Laney was carrying Brody's baby. Slade's job was to protect and care for both of them as Brody would have wanted him to.

No more, no less. Simple as that.

He only wished it felt as clear-cut as it should be. He had to get his act together, and fast, just the way he did before going into the arena. Riding a bull was as much a mental exercise as it was a physical one. He needed to extend the same principles to his friendship with Laney. Keep his wits about him at all times.

When he arrived at the Becketts', Slade first checked the ranch office. That's where he usually found Laney when he came to visit her, sitting behind her desk and up to her cute black reading glasses in paperwork.

He couldn't help but be impressed by how well she'd taken to ranch management—the part of it she could do now, anyway. She'd said she'd worked at a large marketing firm in business management, but running a ranch could hardly require the same skills. Yet she handled it all with grace, picking up on the unfamiliar aspects quickly and competently. And he had the sneaking suspicion that once Baby Beckett was born, Laney would tackle the rest of ranch management with a vengeance, becoming as equally capable on the back of a horse as she was behind the desk.

The office was empty, so Slade went looking for Laney in the house. He shucked his boots and hung up his hat in the mudroom and then started checking for Laney room by room, passing first through the kitchen and then into the dining area. Carol and Grant appeared not to be home and he was beginning to wonder if Laney was absent as well, when he heard the warm Texas lilt of her voice coming from the living room.

"It's only a two and a half hour drive. I'll be fine." There was a pause and then she continued. "I'll stop at least once an hour and get out and stretch. Yes, I promise. My ankles are swollen enough without adding a long, nonstop drive into the mix."

She was going somewhere? How had he not known about that? She hadn't mentioned it to him, but then again, why would she?

Still, wherever she was going for her little day trip, Slade was determined to go with her—to make sure she kept the promises she was making to whomever she was speaking with on the other end of the phone. Two and a half hours one way meant a total of five hours on the road in one day, assuming she was making a round trip in one day. That was an awful lot for a woman in her condition. She might think she was up to it but he didn't want to take any chances.

He rounded the corner just as she pressed the end button on her cell. "I didn't mean to eavesdrop, but I heard you say that you—" His breath left him in a rush when he spotted the two suitcases by the door.

He felt as if he'd been sucker punched.

He tried to inhale but couldn't force air into his lungs.

It was as if all the oxygen had left the room. "You're leaving?"

As in *leaving*, leaving. *No, no, no, no, no.*

"Yes." Her eyebrows arched, surprise clearly written on her expression.

That wasn't much of an answer, and it wasn't anywhere close to what Slade wanted—*needed*—to hear.

"Just like that? You're out of here?"

"Just like that," she repeated with a smile. "Don't worry. Carol and Grant already know I'm going."

Slade's pulse ratcheted. "And they're okay with this?" Surely Brody's parents wouldn't want Laney traipsing all over Texas—or worse yet…

The thought that had first occurred to him when he'd seen her suitcases assaulted him now. What if she was leaving for good?

"Okay with it?" She sounded genuinely surprised. "They were the ones who suggested it."

He felt as if he'd missed something major. He and Laney were evidently talking at cross-purposes. Grant and Carol were sending her away? Sending their *grandchild* away? It didn't make any sense.

Maybe he was the one who'd misinterpreted what was going on. Maybe he was overreacting. Maybe there was a simple answer. He hoped.

"Where are you headed?" He hoped he didn't sound as desperate as he felt, but he was choking on the news that she was leaving. As selfish as it was, he couldn't let her walk out that door, taking Baby Beckett away from him before he or she was even born. There were too many suitcases for it to be a short trip, and the baby was due in a month.

And it wasn't just Baby Beckett whom he stood to

lose. The thought of never seeing Laney again—well, he simply couldn't go there. Not for a second. This was quickly becoming his worst nightmare.

"I'm off to my sister's place in Houston. That's where I lived before coming to Serendipity, you know."

He did know. So what did that mean? Had she changed her mind? Was she going back to live with her sister? What had changed that was causing her to run off to her sister's place?

"You'd give up? Just like that?"

She gaped at him. "What do you mean, *give up*? I can't believe you'd even accuse me of such a thing. Don't you know me well enough by now to know I don't quit at *anything*?"

He did. He *thought* he did.

He shook his head to clear his thoughts, but Laney misinterpreted the gesture as a negative response. Heat rose to her face, staining her cheeks a fierce red. Which would have been pretty, had she not been glaring daggers at him. She clenched her fists and for a moment Slade thought she was going to deck him, but she either decided against it or the movement was merely a way for her to control her temper.

"You can't leave." He knew he was pleading, but for maybe the first time in his life, he put his ego on the back burner for the sake of someone else. Two someone's.

She flared up like a peahen, her feathers clearly ruffled as she invaded his personal space. They were only inches away from each other. He was several inches taller than she so he shouldn't have felt intimidated by the move, but somehow, he did. He'd rather not have to deal with an angry Laney.

"You don't get to tell me what to do, you big oaf. I can't believe it. I thought you'd changed, but you're still the same overbearing jerk you've always been."

He should have been offended, but he was too busy trying to mentally regroup. Her nearness was doing a number on him, stirring his senses. He couldn't think straight over the woodsy scent of her perfume, her glossy full lips—even if they were turned down at the corners—and the sparks emanating from her eyes. For a couple of seconds he completely forgot what they were talking—arguing—about, or that she'd just called him all kinds of names, none of them pleasant.

She wasn't playing fair standing this close to him, although from the harsh expression on her face, he doubted she had any idea of the impact she was having over him.

"I—er—" he stammered, knowing if he didn't get a handle on this conversation, it was going to head right down the garden path, and he had a pretty good idea of how she would respond if he did what he was thinking about doing, which was taking her into his arms and kissing the daylights out of her.

Now *that* would take the wind out of her sails.

It would also probably get him slapped, and rightly so. It would prove her point—that he hadn't really changed at all, falling back on his old habits to get his way. He'd never be able to convince her that the emotions he was experiencing were nothing like anything he'd ever had before in his life, brought on by the threat of her walking out for good.

"You assume the worst of me and think I'm abandoning my responsibilities when you don't even know what you're talking about," she charged, visibly refusing to be cowed by his superior height, not that he was trying to impose on her or take advantage. Not like that, anyway. He didn't dare move any closer, which meant he needed to back off.

Now would be good.

It struck him as humorous that she'd accused him of not knowing what he was talking about. She couldn't possibly know what he was thinking, since the only thing he'd managed to do so far was stutter nonsensically. Wouldn't she be surprised if she knew what was running through his head right now?

Surprised. And angry.

"You're right, princess. I *don't* know. So why don't you enlighten me?" He kept his tone deep and even, knowing the expression of endearment he'd purposefully used would be enough to get her to back off.

Or deck him. That possibility was definitely still on the table.

She growled in frustration and stepped away from him, turning on her heels so her back was to him, then whirling around to face him again. Steam might not be literally coming from her ears, but figuratively, it was doing all that and more. "You. Are. Incorrigible."

He grinned and winked at her. His natural charm usually worked with women, getting him ahead in the conversation. Though he doubted it would work with Laney, he had no other tools to use. "Thank you."

"That wasn't meant to be a compliment. You are the most exasperating man I've ever had the misfortune to meet."

That bad, huh? This whole conversation brought him back to the first time he'd seen her after she'd moved in with the Becketts, wandering around helplessly on the grassy range. Good thing he'd come by then and pointed her toward home. She was clearly as lost now as she'd been then, and it was equally in her favor that he'd come around now, because instead of being determined to make a go of it in Serendipity, she was now apparently set on leaving.

Which he couldn't let her do, obviously. But at this point he wasn't sure how to talk her out of it.

"Why *are* you leaving?" He slumped onto the couch and extended his arm over the back, giving her a little bit of space and hoping it would help her open up and tell him what was really going on, because he still couldn't even begin to guess. He'd thought everything was going so well for her here.

When she didn't budge, he gestured to a nearby softly pillowed armchair, thinking it would be the most comfortable for her. "At least sit down and talk to me about it."

He hoped he didn't sound as clueless and frustrated as he felt. His senses were still on overload and now his mind and heart were, too.

She shook her head and joined him on the couch. "If I sit down in that chair I'll never be able to get out of it again."

"Oh. I didn't think—"

"You wouldn't know. I had no idea how limiting some aspects of late pregnancy are until I experienced them. Sometimes I feel like a beached whale."

"Not even close," he assured her. Was that was this was about? Did she feel she didn't have enough support here? Had handling the stress of the ranch business become too much for her and she was worried about Baby Beckett's health?

If that's all it was, he could handle it. Whatever support she needed to stay on at the Becketts', he could and would provide.

"I'll do anything to help you," he vowed solemnly, placing a hand over his heart. "You just have to ask and I'll be there for you, and for the baby. You don't have to lift a finger if you don't want to. As far as I'm concerned, you can just rest on the couch all day and read your books. I'll take care of everything else, I promise."

"I don't need—" she started, and then stopped, her eyes widening and her jaw slackening. "Oh. So *that's* what this is about. You think I'm leaving permanently. Why didn't you just say that in the first place and save us both all this grief?"

He jerked his chin toward the suitcases by the door, his throat tightening. "Aren't you leaving?"

"No. Yes—but not in the way you mean. I'm just going to visit my sister for a few days before it becomes too cumbersome for me to travel."

Relief flooded through him. He was surprised by the strength of his emotions. *She was coming back. With Baby Beckett.* He didn't even want to examine why his first thought had been of Laney and not the baby.

"I'll be gone for three days."

"With all that luggage? You have to admit that's pretty condemning, two suitcases for three days. You can't blame me for getting the wrong impression."

"I travel prepared for anything."

"I guess."

"So you see, you were worried over nothing. You don't have to worry about me, or about the ranch, for that matter. I'll be back so fast you won't even miss me."

He knew *that* wasn't true, although he wasn't about

to admit it to Laney. He would miss her every day until she returned. He missed her now.

"You promise you'll take it easy driving? And turn around and come back home if you think anything might be amiss?"

Her eyes flashed in surprise when he called the Becketts' ranch her *home*. Had he really just said that aloud, after denying her that satisfaction for as long as she'd been here? Next thing he knew he'd be blurting out all kinds of mortifying thoughts.

"You're as bad as my sister, worrying about every little thing I do. I can take care of myself—and the baby. But yes, I promise you that I'll—"

Her sentence dropped into silence, her expression contorted and she cradled her belly with both hands.

"Laney? Princess? What's wrong?" He had her in his arms in a second, carefully embracing her and supporting her against whatever was happening to her. Whatever it was, she was clearly in pain.

"It's probably nothing," she said, sweeping in a deep breath. Her voice was shaky and unsure.

"It's settled, sweetheart. You can't—" His declaration was immediately cut off when she groaned and tucked her head into his chest.

"It's nothing," she repeated.

Slade didn't believe her, not for one second. And he didn't care one bit if he sounded dictatorial or not. He was taking over, and he was doing it immediately. She could deck him later if she wanted, but at this moment, he was in control.

"I'm taking you to see Dr. D.," he said, his tone brooking no argument. "I'm not going to fight you on this."

She shook her head. At first he thought she was denying his request—demand—but her words both relieved him and frightened him at the same time.

"I'm not fighting you," she said on a sigh. "Please. I think I need to see the doctor. Right away."

Laney had never experienced real labor pains before, and she prayed she was not having real contractions now. She'd read about Braxton Hicks, the practice contractions pregnant women sometimes had, in all of the many pregnancy-related books she'd devoured over the past few months. But she didn't know what those were supposed to feel like, either, only that they mimicked real contractions but weren't as strong or as regular. Since she was still a good month away from her due date, she had reason to be concerned, at least enough to make a visit to Dr. Delia's office. The trip to her sister's house would have to wait.

Not that she had any choice in the matter. She knew how stubborn Slade could be when he got something into his head, and right now, he wasn't about to take no for an answer. He'd bundled her up in a blanket and practically carried her to his truck, even going so far as to buckle her in—as if she'd suddenly forgotten how to use a seat belt.

She probably should have been offended, but his touch was gentle and his expression was lined with concern. Naturally he would be worried. It was his best friend's baby they were talking about here.

Actually, they weren't talking at all. Slade was mumbling something under his breath as he drove, but she couldn't tell what he was saying.

"Are you talking to me?" she asked, checking the

second hand on her watch to time the contractions, which, after the first few, had become further apart and less consistent in length and strength. It was just that first one that had overwhelmed her. She was probably making something out of nothing, but she'd feel better after she'd talked to the doctor. She needed to know for sure that there weren't any problems, and that she wasn't going into premature labor.

"I—" He glanced over at her his hat low and shading his eyes from her perusal. "No. I was talking to God."

"Praying?" She couldn't have been more surprised. Slade was a man of faith? He'd never said anything. The brash, flirtatious cowboy had a personal relationship with God? She was certain she hadn't seen him in church since she'd been in town.

That wasn't really fair to him, though, was it? She was hardly in any position to judge. Maybe he had his own reasons for not attending the church in town. He was out and about many weekends on the rodeo circuit.

She had seen the good in Slade, more than once, in fact, glimpses of a soft heart underneath that gruff exterior of his.

"I know," he admitted with a self-deprecating laugh, filling the silent space. He glanced at her and one side of his mouth kicked up. "You wouldn't think that of me, would you? That God and I could be having a conversation?"

"Well, I—" What was she supposed to say? She *had* been thinking the worst of him, had immediately jumped to the wrong conclusions, just as he suspected she would.

"And you'd be right in your assumptions," he assured her. "Or at least, you would have been, up until a few days before—before—" He stalled and his voice lowered. "Brody had his accident."

Another contraction hit at the same time as Slade's words struck her and she tried not to wince, since seeing her in distress clearly distracted him from the road. She needed him to concentrate on driving.

"Did you grow up in church?" she asked, as much to distract herself as to keep Slade talking. The contractions weren't supposed to be so strong, never mind this fast, were they? This wasn't right. Not with a first baby. It should take her much longer—hours—before she reached this level of pain. She was more worried than she let on but kept her thoughts to herself, mostly because Slade already looked as if he was about to jump out of his skin. Who knew what he would do if she voiced her concerns?

"Absolutely. I was raised in the church." She was grateful that he appeared not to notice any change in her demeanor. "Serendipity is a small town with a big heart. Nearly everyone goes to church, which is part of the reason I haven't worked up the courage to return since I stopped attending as a youth. I haven't exactly been a model Christian. When I hit puberty I rebelled against authority, and that included God. And you of all people know how terribly I behaved as a young adult."

She smiled through the pain. "Now, why am I not surprised that you were a difficult teenager?"

He chuckled but slid her a worried glance, furtively checking on her when he thought she wasn't looking. "You have no idea how much grief I gave my parents. My mother used to say she was going to be bald from pulling her hair out at some of the antics Brody and I got into when we were younger."

"So what brought you back around?" She was more than just curious now, getting a glimpse into a side of Slade she had no idea existed. "To your faith, I mean."

This time when he glanced at her he held her gaze for a few moments. "I'm too ashamed to say. You really don't want to know."

"Hey, if God got your attention, it can't be too bad."

He groaned and jerked his chin. "It was. As bad as it could be, and it was made infinitely worse by the fact that Brody was already married to you at the time."

Suddenly she wasn't sure she wanted to hear this story, but she'd been the one to open this can of worms. Slade had tried to warn her off of it and she hadn't listened.

"I challenged Brody to something I shouldn't have," Slade admitted, his tone muted. "A rodeo princess much like you caught my eye, and I dared him to see who'd be the first man to get her attention. I don't think Brody was in any way interested in the woman. He just couldn't back down from the challenge."

Even after all this time and everything that had changed between them, it still hurt that Slade hadn't respected her marriage to Brody, but she knew he was genuinely regretful of his part in the problems in the relationship. Clearly he had no idea that she hadn't exactly been a rodeo princess—hardly one of those buckle bunnies Slade and Brody must have been used to, the ones they used to chase and who used to chase them.

She was a city girl who'd won a contest sponsored by a local radio station and ended up in the arena on the back of a horse with a crown on her head. She'd never in her life been to a rodeo until the night she'd met Brody, and she hadn't been to one since. The idea of attending the upcoming Serendipity rodeo made her feel sick to her stomach, but now was hardly the time to get into all that. Slade's eyes were on the road, but she could tell he was lost in the past.

"So like I said, we were vying to see which one of us could get her attention first. We were just a couple of arrogant jerks who thought too much of themselves and not enough about the women we were chasing. Imagine our surprise when we tailed her into cowboy church. Let's just say neither one of us was ready for what happened next. We didn't get the woman's attention, but God sure got ours."

"Mmm," she said, not so much an affirmation as it was an expression of pain. Up until this point Slade had been unusually attentive, but now he didn't appear to notice her struggle to breathe evenly through the contraction wracking her midsection.

Conversation ceased as he pulled his truck in front of the doctor's office. It had only been a five minute drive but it had felt much longer than that, not only because of the two contractions she'd experienced while inside the truck, but also because of all Slade had revealed about himself.

"I can walk," she assured him when he rushed around to get her door.

"Be that as it may," he said, gripping her elbow with one hand and securing the other around her waist. "I'm here to help you, and I don't want to take any chances with your health. Or the baby's."

It was a little bit embarrassing to have Slade coddling her as they entered the doctor's office, and she was thankful when Delia didn't make a big deal of it.

"She's having contractions," Slade informed the doctor before Laney could say a word. He actually sounded a little frightened, or at least completely lost. "Dr. D., you've got to do something for her."

Delia gestured to the examination room. Unlike the previous visit where Slade stayed out in the waiting room lumbering around like a grizzly, this time he stayed by Laney's side, helping her onto the table and keeping a firm, reassuring grip on her hand.

"You're just over thirty-six weeks, right?" Delia asked. Laney nodded. Delia smiled reassuringly. "There's no cause for worry, hon. Many healthy babies have been delivered at thirty-six weeks, although ideally we'd like to keep this little bun cooking in the oven for a few weeks longer. Let's get you hooked up to a fetal monitor and see what we're looking at. Then I'll call Zach and Ben and put them on standby with the ambulance, just in case these contractions are the real deal. As you probably know, at thirty-six weeks there's always the possibility that the baby's lungs may not be fully developed. It's nothing to worry about now, but just in case it comes to that, I'd feel more comfortable if you delivered in a hospital setting rather than here."

"Hospital?" Slade repeated, his face blanching and his voice nearly an octave higher than usual. "An ambulance? It's that serious?" He was squeezing Laney's hand so tightly she thought she might be losing circulation in her fingers.

"Slade," she said, brushing her free hand over his. "Isn't it me who is supposed to be squeezing your hand?"

His grip immediately loosened and color returned to his face in spades. He gulped a breath of air. "I'm so sorry, princess."

Delia and Laney shared a laugh at Slade's expense, but he grinned and shrugged it off. He really did look completely out of his element. He was as jumpy as a wet cat, acting even more nervous than Laney felt, which might have rubbed off on her, but thankfully didn't. She found herself enveloped in peace, knowing God would bring Baby Beckett into the world at just the right time and place, whether at the hospital or elsewhere, now or nearer to the due date.

Slade was definitely not in the same emotional space as she was. *Peace* wasn't even close to the word she would use to describe him right now. He'd removed his hat when he'd entered the office and had scrubbed his fingers through his hair so many times that the black tips were sticking up every which direction. His electric blue eyes held an untamed quality to them, as though he was a wild animal ready to break from his cage.

He was definitely worried, that much she'd give him. She couldn't help but wonder what the basis of his actions were all about.

Was he worried about Baby Beckett, or did his concern extend to her, as well? Maybe he was simply experiencing a lingering sense of guilt on his part for what had happened between him and Brody, especially since they'd just been talking about it. His story about leading Brody down the wrong path certainly explained a lot—just not enough to satisfy her.

What if that was all it was—some lingering sense of responsibility toward her and Baby Beckett? She was grateful for his help, and his motives shouldn't matter.

But they did.

Another contraction started just as the realization washed over her—she *did* care what Slade thought of her. The intensity of this contraction was weaker than the last. The raw, coarse tightening of her chest around her heart felt infinitely more painful than any contraction could be.

How had she managed to put herself in this position? She'd lost her focus, which should be on the blessing of life, God's beautiful gift residing within her, not to mention all she had to learn to keep Brody's ranch, his legacy to his child, intact.

Definitely not on Slade.

After a while Delia returned and checked the tape dangling from the fetal monitor, nodding at the peaks and valleys where Laney's contractions had occurred.

"Good news," Delia said, patting Laney on the shoulder.

Slade's grip on her hand tightened again, but she didn't bother reminding him about it. She was too busy holding her breath.

"I don't think you're in labor," Delia continued. "I know the contractions feel strong to you—painful, even—but they aren't registering particularly high or regularly on the monitor, which I would expect to see if you were in real labor. I'm fairly certain this is just a practice run."

Laney chuckled weakly. Of course she was relieved by the news, but she was more than a little overwhelmed by it all.

"If this is just practice, I hate to imagine what the real thing will be like," she said, trying to laugh off her misgivings and utterly failing. She was frightened. Who wouldn't be? It was her first baby and she didn't have any idea what to expect. And yet women had been giving birth since the beginning of time. She'd make it through whatever was thrown at her.

Slade jumped in before Delia could speak. "There are painkillers or something she can use, right? Some way to make it easier for her during labor?"

Delia nodded, amusement evident in her gaze and the quirk of her lips. "Don't worry, Slade. Laney has plenty of options at her disposal when the time comes. I'm sure she's educated herself in all of this, and she'll have plenty of help around her, whether here or at a hospital. She'll be able to keep her labor pains manageable."

Laney did know all about those options, everything ranging from narcotics to epidurals, but she didn't plan to use anything to manage her pain. Despite her unexpected and surprisingly painful introduction to contractions, she wanted to have a natural birth. But seeing the concern lining Slade's face, she didn't think now would be a good time to bring that up, especially as relieved as he'd appeared once he heard there were ways to ease her pain in labor. She could actually see the muscles in his neck and shoulders unwinding.

"I want you to take it easy for a couple of days, Laney," Delia instructed. "Slade, make sure she doesn't take on too much, okay?"

"Yes, ma'am," he answered with a firm jerk of his chin, his gaze as serious as Laney had ever seen it. "I promise I'm not going to let her lift a finger."

Laney sighed. There went her trip to see her sister. She knew Slade well enough to know he wasn't going to let her out of his sight until he deemed her well and fully past this trial. She doubted if he'd even let her off the couch to do anything more strenuous than visiting the bathroom.

If he was this assertive now, she couldn't even begin to imagine how bad he'd be once the baby was born.

The thought made her smile. For all his domineering behavior, she wouldn't change him if she could. His single-minded focus and his strength were what made him the man he was. She hated to admit it, but his overbearing attitude more often than not seemed to originate from his need to *do* something, to fix whatever appeared to him as a problem. In Slade's world, mountains weren't for looking at—they had to be conquered.

Maybe that was what had gone wrong in her marriage to Brody, she realized, as Slade wrapped her in a blanket and bundled her back out to the truck, fussing over her as if she was made of fine china and might break at any moment.

Now that the thought had occurred to her, she couldn't help but compare Slade with Brody. From the moment she and Brody had exchanged vows, she had done nothing but try to change him. She'd been attracted to the young, handsome bull rider, and yet she'd never accepted the rodeo as part of his life, nor the fact that he served on the police force. Had she simply embraced who he was and not tried to make into something he wasn't, maybe things would have been different. He might have taken her with him to his weekend rodeos, or brought her home to Serendipity.

Brody was a risk-taker and a thrill-seeker. That was who he'd been, and she'd had no business trying to mold him into anything other than that. Wasn't it God's job to work on people's hearts?

And the worst part was, she had the evidence right

in front of her that God could work on a man's heart, no matter how hardened he appeared to be on the outside. She remembered Slade saying that the Lord had touched Brody, and Brody had been planning on coming home to her.

She slid a glance at Slade, but his attention was on the road, his hat pulled low over his eyes so she couldn't read what he was thinking. His jaw was tight with strain again, and she couldn't help but wonder what he was thinking that made him look so tense. She'd been proclaimed good to go. She'd expect he'd be relieved by that.

Whatever it was that was bothering him, he obviously didn't feel inclined to share it with her, and she didn't know how to ask, so they rode in silence. Thankfully, her contractions appeared to have petered out. That was one blessing.

It was only after they'd arrived back at the Becketts' ranch and he'd ushered her inside that he spoke. His agitation had faded like the calm after a thunderstorm, at least until it was replaced by his usual dictatorial attitude, the one she knew and loved.

Okay, not *loved*. But at least it was familiar.

"You," he said, pointing first to her and then to the sofa. "There. Now. I'm going to go find you some extra pillows. When I get back, I expect to see you lying down with your feet up. Understood?"

"Bully," she muttered.

"Stubborn woman," he replied back, one corner of his mouth lifting.

They were both right, Laney thought. As evenly matched as two people could be. It was a toss-up to know who would prevail, or even if it were possible for either of them to win at their constant battle of wills.

She didn't even know if it mattered, because at this point she wasn't entirely sure she wanted to win.

Chapter Nine

Slade was fairly satisfied with what he'd accomplished. He'd managed to keep Laney comfortable and resting—for the most part, anyway. When he'd called her stubborn, he'd had no idea just how true his observation was. It had been the longest five days of his life, trying to keep Laney resting on the couch.

From the moment her fake contractions—or whatever they were called—diminished, the woman had been just itching to get up and back to work. It was all Slade could do to keep her contained.

Naturally, he had stopped her from taking that kind of risk, with Grant and Carol's assistance. And it hadn't been easy.

Doctor's orders. And he would keep telling her that until she actually listened to him. He'd completely cleared his schedule so he could be with her. One of the benefits of small-town living—the police captain was a personal friend and was very understanding about his needing time off.

He wasn't about to let anything happen to Laney or Baby Beckett, even if that meant sitting with her for hours on end and bringing her all her meals on a tray. She'd teased him about being her own personal maid, but he didn't care what she called him, as long as she stayed put.

Even though he still felt awkward about expressing his faith, they'd prayed together about Baby Beckett's health. He privately amended his own petitions to ask God to also protect Laney. He was only now beginning to realize how deep her faith went, and it nudged at his heart. He would do well to emulate her in that regard. While he was still struggling with the basics, she'd learned how to lean on God through the worst of it, the school of hard knocks with Brody's death and then all the opposition the world could possibly have thrown at her.

His opposition, to be precise.

He was ashamed to realize just how much grief he'd caused this sweet, special woman. Pushing Brody to ignore his wedding vows. Putting up every possible roadblock when Laney had first moved to Serendipity. He couldn't have acted like a bigger jerk if that was intentionally what he'd set out to be.

After five straight days of bed rest, Laney was champing at the bit to get out for, as she put it, some much-needed fresh air. Slade wasn't entirely convinced she wouldn't be pushing herself too hard, but with Serendipity's annual rodeo only a week and a half away, Slade had a ton of things he had to accomplish and little time to do it all. Yet he was determined not to leave Laney's side for an instant, so he found himself in a bit of a conundrum.

He'd offered to help set up for the event, which was held at the public stable arena. Folks from small towns all around the area would be out for the event and the arena would be at full capacity. Bleachers had to be set up and equipment needed to be tested, not to mention the fact that while he'd been watching over Laney, he hadn't been preparing for his ride. So in the end he'd given in to Laney's nagging and was taking her out to the arena. Killing two birds with one stone, and all that.

He wouldn't ride a bull in front of her. Not until he had to, even if the bull in question was a practice bull and far beneath his skill set. There were plenty of other things to keep him busy, and some time outside would no doubt raise Laney's spirits.

Seemed like a good compromise, but as he kicked back on the Becketts' armchair waiting for Laney to get ready, he once again considered the wisdom of taking her out, especially to the arena. He hadn't mentioned again to her his intention to ride in the rodeo, and he wasn't sure how she was going to react upon discovering he was sticking to his original plans. He wasn't even sure how to approach the subject, so they hadn't ever discussed it. The last thing she needed was to experience any stress or strain right now.

He wasn't sure how to break the news to her, but after careful consideration, he realized the best way for him to handle it would be to come right out and tell her. It would be far more shocking for her to discover he was riding on the day of the event than if he was honest with her to begin with. That didn't make it any easier to figure out what to say, though.

He'd invited her to the arena today with the intention of coming clean, and of gently acclimating her to being around the rodeo and all it entailed. She hadn't been back to a rodeo since Brody's death and he was half surprised when she accepted his invitation. The whole idea of being at a rodeo had to be difficult for her. In many ways, it was for him as well, but he had a good reason for overcoming his reluctance—to honor Brody.

He didn't know how many rodeos she'd attended prior to meeting him and Brody, but he expected there had been many, as pretty and talented as she was. Who *wouldn't* choose her to be a rodeo princess?

He'd even put her name in the hat for the Serendipity rodeo. She wouldn't be able to race around the arena on the back of a horse, but surely the powers that be could make some kind of exception for her—take her around in the back of a truck, maybe. Some sparkles and a sash and it wouldn't matter how she entered the arena. All eyes would be on her.

"You ready?" He jumped to his feet, hat in hand, as she came down the hallway and out into the living room.

He couldn't remember her ever looking so beautiful, sporting blue jeans and an emerald Western shirt that stretched tightly over her midsection. She was an attractive woman and pregnancy had done nothing to detract from that, but it wasn't the way she was dressed that made Slade's breath catch in his throat.

She was glowing. Her eyes glittered with excitement and her cheeks flushed a pretty rose underneath his intense scrutiny.

"Good enough?" She followed the question with a short, self-conscious laugh.

Good enough? Try great. Amazing. Outstanding. Gorgeous.

But the only thing that came out of his mouth was a

strangled groan. All he could do was nod like an idiot and hope she knew what he meant.

"I was going to go for a sundress, since the spring weather has been so beautiful, but then I got to thinking that the arena has a dirt surface and there might be cowboys on horses kicking up dust."

And bulls. Their eyes met but neither one of them voiced the thought aloud.

"You look mighty fine just the way you are, princess." At least his ability to speak actual English words had returned. That was a relief, but he still felt as awkward as a teenage boy on his first date—not that this was a date.

So why did he feel so self-conscious, tongue-tied and gangly? Heat flooded through him from the tip of his boots to the top of his head.

Wonderful. It wasn't as if she wouldn't notice him turning cherry red.

She grinned at him, the sparkle in her brown eyes suggesting she saw right through him. So much for her not seeing the obvious.

"Why Slade McKenna, was that a compliment?" She sounded like a regular Southern belle, which only served to make him want to twitch around like a million tiny ants were crawling all over him. He'd never been so uncomfortable in his life.

Try as he might, he couldn't seem to regain command of his wayward wits and his senses were shattering every which direction. He curled the brim of his hat in his fist, desperate to regain a modicum of control, searching for a way to speak without sounding like a muddleheaded youth.

In the end he decided the easiest route out of the corner in which he'd trapped himself would be to blurt out the truth. He did find her attractive. And maybe if he teased her, it would have the added benefit of turning their attention back to her instead of on him.

"Yes, ma'am. It was a compliment, and well-deserved. Now let's get out of here before your head swells to the size of your belly."

"Oh, you." She slapped his shoulder playfully. "But seriously, thank you for taking me out of the house. I couldn't stand one more second being cooped up inside."

"Just don't overdo it," he said, rushing to open the screen door for her before she could do it herself.

"You worry too much. How am I going to overexert myself? I know you. You'll have an eye on me every single second of the day."

"You'd better believe it," he agreed, still feeling slightly reluctant about the whole outing. "I'll have a couple of the men help me spread out a tent awning to cover the bleachers to shade you and the baby from the sun."

"You think of everything. All you're going to let me do is sit on the bleachers and watch you, right? What possible harm could come to me or Baby Beckett?" She laughed. "Although I doubt Baby is too worried about sunburn at the moment."

"True." His heart warmed that she'd said she would be watching. He hoped *he* was the man she'd be watching. His mind fled back to the jam session and how many of the single cowboys there had flocked to her side and tried to get her attention. He didn't want her eye wandering to any of those guys.

The first thing he did when he arrived at the stable

was to find a couple of guys to help him set up Laney under an awning, as promised. Once she was seated, he jogged back to his truck to retrieve a cooler he'd filled with fruit and cold water.

"You don't have to fuss over me," she admonished gently. "Really. This is too much, Slade."

"No such thing."

She patted the spot next to her on the bleachers. "I know you have a lot to do today, but sit with me for a moment."

Her gaze turned serious and her brow lowered. His heart thudded wildly and then ground to a sudden halt.

"You're still planning to ride a bull, aren't you?"

He choked on an answer he wasn't yet prepared to give and tensed for the opposition he felt sure was coming.

Instead, she nodded and shifted her gaze away from him, staring off to somewhere on the other side of the arena. She was silent for a long moment before speaking.

"I figured."

He raised his eyebrows in surprise. She could have knocked him over with a single finger to the chest. "You did?"

"You're a bull rider. What else would you do?"

He could ride a horse—be a bullfighter for other riders. He could rope or steer wrestle. He could bow out completely, for that matter, and that was exactly what he'd expected her to suggest to him. Who could blame her?

She didn't sound mad. Why wasn't she mad?

"You're not angry?"

She shifted her gaze to him and shook her head. "I

can't say it doesn't bother me. Obviously I have reason to fear the sport, and I'll be praying for you every single second of your ride. But it would be ridiculous to expect you to give up something that brings you so much pleasure just because I don't happen to like it."

That got Slade thinking. He'd ridden a dozen practice bulls in preparation for the Serendipity rodeo, but not because he enjoyed it. Riding bulls had lost its flavor for him. Even though Brody had been a skilled rider and the accident that killed him had been a fluke, the whole sport no longer sat well with Slade now that it reminded him of the loss of his dearest friend. He found himself looking at the sport in a whole new light.

No, that wasn't quite right.

Not the sport. He was looking at *himself* differently. Chasing after pretty women, elusive titles and negligible purses was no longer for him. It was for other, younger men. Men who weren't thinking about their lives, their futures.

With the intensity of a sudden punch in the gut, Slade realized he wanted much more—things he'd never given much thought to but was now desperate for. And his new goals were no easier to aspire to, much less gain, than succeeding as a bull rider. Much harder, even.

He wanted the titles of husband and father. Titles Brody had had—or would have had, had he lived to see his baby born.

And Laney...

If Brody had lived, she would have had the protection and stability of the family she deserved. Slade had taken that from her when he'd pushed Brody into riding Night Terror. He'd ruined everything for her.

As for him, he had no right to complain about his

sudden loneliness or to expect any better. It was almost ironic. The fly-by-night life of a bull rider no longer appealed to him, no longer held the attraction it once had. He'd grown up, but it was too late to make things right.

Brody would probably have had a good laugh at his change of heart. His friend would have teased him mercilessly about his sudden desire to man up and settle down.

Or maybe he would have been angry. He had every right to have been, although it hadn't been Brody's style to hold a grudge. Slade had disrespected Brody's relationship with Laney in every possible regard. It made him sick just to think about it. He'd always figured Brody had tagged along with him because he had the same view of relationships. It was disconcerting to imagine that his best buddy might have been going against his conscience all that time. Despite the seeming hastiness of his marriage, Brody had been miles ahead of him in many regards. How many times had Brody tried to explain his change of heart and Slade had not listened, but instead had pressed his friend to continue his delinquent behavior?

Slade wished with all his heart he could change the past. How was it possible that Brody had died while he had lived? In Slade's mind it was the ultimate in unfairness and a perpetual struggle for him. He'd probably never know why God had done what He'd done, taken Brody when He had.

"Whoa. I lost you." Laney bumped his shoulder with hers. "Where'd you go? Your expression turned so dark and ominous there for a second."

"I was thinking about Brody."

"Hard not to, all things considered. He's been on my mind, as well."

"Yeah." His voice was scratchy and rough with strain.

"But you know, the memories aren't all bad. I met Brody at a rodeo. It was the only one I've ever attended, I'm afraid. You'll have to school me in the fine points of the sport so I know what to look for when I'm cheering for you."

She'd be cheering? For *him*? He swallowed hard to dislodge the emotion clogging in his throat.

"Wait—what? The night you met Brody—are you trying to tell me that was your first rodeo? But you were—"

"The rodeo princess. Ironic, isn't it? I won a contest sponsored by a local radio station. I was no more a rodeo *anything* than you are an astronaut. Go figure."

She hadn't even known what she'd signed up for when she'd started her whirlwind romance with Brody. She hadn't been a buckle bunny on the hunt for a bull rider. She couldn't have imagined what her life was going to be like.

"I—I'm sorry, princess. So sorry."

Laney meant her remark to be funny, but Slade didn't look particularly amused. In fact, he appeared downright grumpy, scowling and adjusting the brim of his hat lower over his eyes, which she'd learned over the past few weeks was a tell for him when he was trying to mask his thoughts.

What had she said that had set him off? Why was he saying he was sorry? For what?

She should be the one feeling uncomfortable here, and not just because she was sitting on aluminum bleachers, which would be an unpleasant experience even if she wasn't over eight months pregnant and feeling as if she was ready to pop at any second.

She'd jumped at the chance to come with Slade, and not just because she desperately needed to get out of the house and get some fresh air, which was the excuse she'd given him. There was so much more to it than that, though she didn't know if she could put her feelings into words Slade would understand.

She needed to be here today to watch Slade practice on the back of a bull, to prepare her heart for the real rodeo. She'd known that he was going to compete, even if she still didn't understand exactly why he did what he did.

For about one second she'd considered begging off and not attending the rodeo at all, but if she gave in to her fear it would never leave her. She planned on making Serendipity her home, and the rodeo was a big part of it.

Today was her emotional trial run. After she'd last seen Slade on a bull, he had explained to her that the animal hadn't been anywhere close to the skill level he was used to riding. Practice bulls were to perfect technique. The rodeos were the real challenges. He'd assured her that even the most high-flying, no-holds-barred bull riders didn't want to get injured and disqualify themselves from the true competition.

But just now they hadn't been talking about bulls. They'd been discussing rodeo princesses, or rather the fact that she wasn't technically the real deal. While that information might have come as a surprise, she could hardly see why it would make any kind of difference to him.

"You want to tell me why you clammed up?" she asked. "I was only kidding about you being an astronaut. I'm sure you'd make a splendid moonwalker."

He swallowed a chuckle despite his scowling demeanor.

"I was just thinking about your situation," he responded in a carefully measured tone. "You weren't traveling from rodeo to rodeo like many of the ladies did. You probably didn't know the first thing about bull riding. About bull riders."

"Well, that's true enough. I *still* don't know anything about the rodeo, other than what you've told me. But I fail to see why that would upset you, or what difference it really makes in the big scheme of things."

"You met Brody and he swept you off your feet. You didn't have any idea what you were signing up for when you married him. It's difficult enough being a cop's wife, much less the spouse of a man who lives the life of a cowboy on the rodeo circuit on weekends."

"It wasn't easy," she admitted. "To be honest, I didn't understand Brody's passion for the sport at all. But then again, I never really tried to understand. I didn't talk to him about it, or try to see his perspective. I just knew that the sport scared me, so I pressured him to drop it, and couldn't understand why he refused. I didn't give him the credit he deserved, either. Maybe if I hadn't pushed him so hard to change, he wouldn't have rebelled and done the exact opposite of what I expected out of him."

"You can't put the blame for Brody's actions on yourself. Brody was his own man. If anything, you can land that culpability squarely on my shoulders. I wasn't a good influence by any meaning of the word. If his accident was anybody's fault, it was mine."

"What's past is past. Neither one of us can change what was. We can only strive to do better going forward. That's what Brody would have wanted."

"We agree on that point." He reached for her hand. "Next weekend, when I ride, I just want you to know it will be for the last time."

She couldn't help the sense of relief that flooded through her. Despite her brave words about understanding his desire to ride, she couldn't stand the thought of him getting hurt. Not just because of what had happened to Brody, but because if anything happened to Slade, she wasn't sure what she would do.

Unlike her sudden, fiery relationship with Brody, which lit up like a shooting star and then just as quickly fell to earth, her feelings for Slade had grown over the past few weeks, sneaking up on her and surprising her with their intensity. It was hard for her to believe she couldn't even stand to be near him when they'd first met, but now...

Now she *needed* him in her life. In the baby's life.

If he got hurt—or worse...

She simply couldn't go there, any more than she could let herself consider where her feelings for Slade were leading her.

"I can't say I'm sorry to hear it will be your last ride," she admitted, laying her free hand on his forearm. "But do you mind me asking why?"

"I'm not getting any younger. A man can't ride bulls forever. It's time for me to move on to new challenges."

His answer didn't completely satisfy her, but she

wasn't sure if it was because it didn't quite ring true, or if it was the pained expression in his gaze that stopped her short.

He cleared his throat and looked away from her, ostensibly turning his attention toward the bucking gates, where a Serendipity cowboy she didn't recognize was preparing to ride. Then he covered his hand with hers and she knew he wasn't really paying attention to the cowboy's ride.

"There's something you need to know." She heard the intensity of his voice and unconsciously stiffened. He squeezed her hand, acknowledging the unspoken tension between them.

"It's about Brody's last ride."

"We don't have to rehash that. I know all about it," she assured him around the catch in her voice. "Probably more than I ever wanted to know. Anyway, it doesn't change anything to talk about it."

The baby landed a firm kick on the inside of her ribs and she slid one of her hands from his and rubbed the spot where Baby Beckett's little heel was lodged.

"You don't know everything."

She inhaled, trying to steady her nerves, and sat in silence, not knowing why he continued to push the issue. What good would it do?

When he didn't look at her or continue his thought, she gently probed him. Her mind rebelled against whatever else Slade was about to say. She was relatively certain she didn't want to hear what was coming next, but she knew she couldn't jump off this train now, however fast it was moving.

"Slade?"

"Brody wasn't going to ride that night."

"He wasn't?" That *was* news to her.

"He was anxious to get home. All he could think about after his change of heart at the cowboy church was how much he wanted to see you, to ask for your forgiveness and to do everything he could to repair your marriage."

"I know he was coming home to me. You told me that weeks ago, and it gives my heart great solace. But you're going to tell me why he decided to ride that night instead of walking away from it, aren't you? Whether I want to hear it or not."

She didn't want to do this. She didn't want to go where Slade was leading her. Her emotions were all over the place and she didn't want to keep revisiting the if onlys.

"Yes, I am going to tell you, because you need to know, and you need to hear it from me." He paused and coughed to clear his throat, but his voice still came out husky, miserable and self-accusatory. "It was me. I pushed him to ride that night. I kept reminding him of the purse he'd win if he got a good ride. How great it would be for him to be able to take a little money home to you when he went to see you."

"I don't care about money." She couldn't believe he'd even thought such a thing.

"I know that—now," he said bitterly. "Even then, I don't think I really believed the prize would make a difference to you when I encouraged him to make that ride. He drew the best bull on the circuit and I wanted to see him get those eight seconds."

"Best bull meaning the worst one."

He shrugged and stared down at their intertwined hands. "Yeah."

"And that's what you are hoping to do next weekend? Draw the worst-best bull?"

He winced and still wouldn't look her in the eyes, but it was the fact that he hesitated a beat too long that closed off her breath.

"Yes." He groaned. "Laney, don't. Don't push it."

"What?" No way was she backing down at this point, not with the sense of dread crawling into her chest and twisting itself into painful knots.

What was he not saying?

"Please don't make me continue. If I keep going with this, we're both going to regret it. I'm afraid I'm going to upset you or the baby, and that is the last thing I want to do."

"You started it."

"I had to let you know what kind of man I really am. But please—let's talk about something else now. You just got out of the woods with those—fake contractions."

"No." She didn't know whether this kind of stress could spiral her into labor, but at this point not knowing would be as bad as if Slade just spit it out and revealed whatever it was that he was holding back. She was in too deep to back out now.

"You haven't told me everything. Come clean to me, Slade. Better I find out now than later."

He shook his head. "I don't know about that."

What could he possibly say to her that he believed would be worse than what he'd already said? Truth be told, nothing Slade had admitted had really shocked her. And though she knew he blamed himself for Brody's death, she didn't share that sentiment. Granted, he might have exerted a little friendly influence on Brody, but ultimately it had been Brody's decision to ride that bull. Surely Slade knew that.

He dropped his hand from hers and removed his hat, tunneling his fingers through his thick black hair. He stared down at his Stetson for a moment, curling the brim in his fist.

"Night Terror will be at the rodeo next week."

Night Terror.

The bull that had smashed Brody into a wall, killing him instantly. Her breath left her in a whoosh and her heart slammed into her throat. She gasped for air and her head swirled. She was afraid for a moment that she might be physically ill.

Slade didn't appear to notice, or else he was too far gone to stop his words.

"I want to be the man to ride him."

Laney wanted to shake some sense into the stubborn cowboy. "How could you even consider such a thing?"

"I—I—" he stammered.

She jumped in before he could finish his answer. "They didn't—I mean—how is Night Terror still being used on the circuit? I would think that after—" Her throat closed around the words and she couldn't continue.

"He's a young bull, and a well-bred rodeo bull is worth thousands of dollars. Besides, what happened to Brody wasn't Night Terror's fault. It was a freak accident."

"Be that as it may—" She wrapped her arms protectively over her midsection, her pulse feeling like lead in her veins, and she wondered if she looked as pale as she felt.

"I knew I shouldn't have said anything." His frown

turned to a scowl, but she had the feeling he was turning his anger inward.

Still—she had to know.

"What if I asked you not to ride?"

Chapter Ten

What if I asked you not to ride?

The question had been haunting Slade ever since Laney had asked him, especially since those were the last words she'd spoken to him in over a week. He knew he should have kept his big mouth shut, and this was proof positive of what a total jerk he was.

He couldn't answer her when she'd asked that question because he couldn't tell her what she wanted to hear. He'd walked away without another word.

Laney had been avoiding him for the entire week and a half that followed, and he couldn't blame her, nor could he say he'd made much of an effort to cross paths with her, either. If he were totally honest with himself, he didn't want to know what she thought of him. In her present state of mind, knowing what she knew about him now, she'd be more dangerous to confront than a penned-up wildcat.

Not that he could blame her. If he had that day to do over again he would have kept his trap closed and excused himself to go set up bleachers or check the sound system or something. Anything to get away from the truth.

At least she hadn't gone into premature labor because of his serious lapse in judgment. As much as he wanted to see Baby Beckett, he didn't want the little tyke entering the world too soon.

Maybe it was better that the scene had played out the way it had. It would be better for both Laney and the baby if he just stayed away from them permanently, no matter how much his heart would ache to be separated from them. How ironic was it that he'd finally matured enough to put other people's needs ahead of his own, and that meant he had to stay away from them, even when it hurt him to do so? That he was the very worst thing that could happen to the two people who meant the most to him? And yet how could he do less for the woman he'd come to deeply respect and care for?

She deserved better than that. Better than him.

Despite the overwhelming compulsion to honor Brody's life with this ride, in the past week he'd considered scrapping the rodeo completely more times than he could count. But it was too late to back out now, even if he wanted to, with only two hours before the rodeo was set to begin.

He and a few other bull riders from several nearby towns were waiting to draw their bulls. Slade couldn't stand still waiting for the news. He paced back and forth, tapping his hat against his thigh. The caged movement brought his thoughts back to the day he'd first brought Laney in to see Dr. D. He'd been so nervous for her—for Baby Beckett—that he'd prowled around like a tiger.

That was before he'd known what a wonderful lady

Laney was. How he could have ever thought anything different about her he'd never know. He must have been blind.

As far as he knew, Laney hadn't left the Becketts' ranch in the past week. Hopefully no news was good news. If he wasn't mistaken, it was still too early for Baby Beckett to make an entrance into the big, wide world, but surely Grant or Carol would have called him had Brody's baby already been born.

He was half hoping Laney would decide not to attend the rodeo at all, but he knew her too well to really believe she'd avoid it. Whatever she thought about him riding, she had her own mountains to climb, and scale them she would, with the same strength she used to face the rest of her adversities. He had no doubt about that. Living in fear wasn't Laney's style, and she was the toughest woman he'd ever had the privilege of knowing.

"McKenna." Captain Ian James, Serendipity's police chief and the rodeo announcer, broke into his thoughts. "Where are you, son?"

"Sorry, sir."

"You pulled Night Terror."

Ice coursed through Slade's veins. This was exactly what he wanted. It was exactly what he didn't want.

Ian grabbed his elbow, pulled him aside and bent his head in close, out of the hearing range of the other riders. "You can back out, Slade. None of the other guys will give you any guff if you want to pull another lot. If they say anything, they'll answer to me."

Maybe they would, and maybe they wouldn't. Cowboys were a hard lot. Slade knew how he would have reacted when he was younger. He might not have said anything to the guy's face, but he definitely would have been laughing behind the man's back for displaying such a lack of courage.

Then again, most of these cowboys were friends and neighbors and less likely to judge. They'd known Brody, attended his funeral, grieved for him.

Not that it mattered one way or another. Slade didn't care about what the other cowboys thought of him, whether or not he lost or gained their respect. He was riding in honor of Brody, and there were only three living people whose opinion he cared about.

Grant, Carol and Laney.

"I'm in," he said, so low that Ian had to lean his ear closer in order to hear his response.

"What was that?"

"I'm in." His voice was stronger now that his decision had been made.

It was what he'd wanted, wasn't it? What he'd been thinking about all these months? The chance to best Night Terror, have the ride of his life and end his bull riding career the way he'd started it—and in Brody's name and honor.

He was experiencing a great deal of pent-up energy now that he knew he was going to ride, but it wasn't the same as before. He no longer carried the wild, youthful—and often foolish—confidence and drive he'd once had, but he had something infinitely better.

Maturity. And hope for the future.

No matter how this played out, whether he rode for one second or eight, he would be there for Laney and the baby. He might only be relegated to an honorary Uncle Slade, but he'd take whatever Laney gave him and be thankful for it.

And if he had to daily confront his own feelings,

never allowing them off the back burner no matter how painful it might be for him, then so be it.

He took a short walk to calm his nerves and prepare his mind for the ride ahead of him. He knew he needed to be concentrating on the now and not what might or might not be a very bleak future ahead of him, but it was difficult to keep his thoughts on point.

Very difficult, when Laney's sweet face kept floating into his thoughts, distracting him.

When he returned to the arena, spectators were pouring in, not only from Serendipity, but from several neighboring towns. He hoped Laney would find a comfortable place to sit, somewhere out of the sun.

It would be better for *him* if she didn't come at all, because he wasn't certain he could give Night Terror his full focus knowing Laney was looking on. The last thing she needed was the possibility of watching the same kind of mishap that had killed her husband because Slade wasn't paying attention to his ride.

But she'd be there. He knew it with a certainty he'd rather not have had.

Maybe if he didn't actually see her, didn't know for sure she was there, he would fare better. If he discovered afterward that she had seen him ride—well, he would deal with that eventuality when the time came.

He pulled his hat low over his brow and kept his eyes on the path before him.

Don't look up. Don't look up. Don't look up.

He walked quickly and steadily to the rhythm of his silent mantra.

And then he looked up.

Right into the eyes of Laney Beckett. Of course he'd had to go and look at her, sitting right in the center of one of the bleachers and well under the awning, thankfully. Grant and Carol sat on one side of her and Jo and Frank Spencer on the other, protectively sandwiching her in their love.

Maybe if he just kept walking...

But Laney had seen him. He couldn't very well not acknowledge her, especially since it appeared she'd been intently watching him, maybe for some time now.

Of course she had.

The moment their gazes met, his legs stopped working of their own accord. He might as well have been frozen in ice. He couldn't move a muscle. His whole body deserted him at the worst possible time.

He couldn't breathe. Couldn't blink.

She waved, but it was a jerky motion. She paled and dropped her arm, then leaned in to whisper in Carol's ear.

Carol smiled and nodded as Laney rose to her feet and began tenuously making her way to the edge of the bleachers, where she could ostensibly climb down, were she not ridiculously pregnant. The bleachers made for shaky stadium seating at best and not anywhere near safe enough for Laney to be crawling around up there.

Heat burned through him, instantly melting his deep freeze. He didn't even think about his next move. Instinctively, he tucked his head and ran for all he was worth, reaching the bleachers just as she crossed to the edge.

Her eyes widened when he put his arms up to catch her. She was only a few feet from the ground, but it was too far for her to jump on her own in her condition. Her only other option was to pick her way step by step through a crowd of people.

He smiled and nodded his encouragement to her. She shook her head and her full lips curved up at the corners, but it was the glint in her wide eyes that communicated without words how crazy she thought his antics were.

So she thought it was a terrible idea. What was new? She always thought his ideas were bad. Too bad, because it was happening. He might not be able to do anything about her state of mind during the bull ride, but he could see her safely to the ground right now.

He would never let this woman down again.

"Come on, princess," he said, stretching his arms even higher. She could practically lean down and touch him if she tried.

But it wasn't about that. Not for him, and not for her.

It was about trust.

It reminded him of a game he'd played in his high school psychology class. Teammates had had to take turns falling backward into the other's arms. The whole point was knowing their partners would be there to catch them.

Trust.

Of course, at the time, he'd dipped his partner—a cute girl—nearly to the floor and then swept her back up again at the very last second, making her scream and squeal when she thought she was going to hit the ground. But he hadn't let her fall.

Hadn't happened then, and most certainly wouldn't happen now.

Laney narrowed her gaze on him and planted her fists on her hips. "You'd better catch me, mister."

He grinned up at her, and for one second he was

completely in the moment, thinking neither of his past or of the ride to come.

Only Laney, with her beautiful chocolate-brown eyes and ready smile and a laugh that would make any man weak in the knees.

"Are you gonna jump, princess, or am I gonna have to come up after you?"

She didn't hesitate any longer, but launched herself into his arms. He'd expected to catch her under her shoulders and set her quickly and gently to the ground, but somehow they got all tangled up in each other—arms, legs and baby bump. Her face was buried in his chest, right next to his rapidly beating heart. His nose brushed across her hair. It was impossible not to breathe in the alluring woodsy scent of her perfume.

Every thought left his head and he knew if he didn't step away immediately—running away might be the safer choice—he would succumb to the inevitable and make a huge spectacle of both himself and Laney, in a crowd of people so dense they would have no possible chance of getting away with it unnoticed. And in a town like Serendipity, it only took one person's observation for gossip to spread like a Texas grass fire.

He stumbled back, intent on getting a handle on his emotions before they led him far astray, but she reached for his hand, gripping it tightly as she pulled him to a more private spot behind the bleachers.

Bad idea, going behind the bleachers. A very, *very* bad idea.

Laney had no way of knowing Slade's reputation for his "youthful indiscretions" behind the bleachers back in high school, but if she kept this up, she was about to find out.

Up close and personal.

And then she'd deck him, no doubt. He'd had it coming for a long while now.

Could he help it if every nerve ending in his body was crackling? If his senses were swimming, stealing both his breath and his thoughts away from him?

All he could manage was to try to grasp what little was left of his sanity and hope that she couldn't hear the rapid pounding of his heart. His pulse was roaring in his ears so he didn't know how Laney could possibly not be aware of it, especially when she turned to him and laid her palm on his chest, right over his heart.

She gazed up at him, smiling softly, and he saw an impish sparkle in her gaze that could only mean—

She didn't. She couldn't.

Not with him.

He must be misinterpreting the signs. This wasn't the right time or place. And he wasn't the right man for her. He could never be. And the baby—even if he and Laney could ever work out, it would never be about them alone. They both had Brody's baby to consider, and not as an afterthought.

They'd both loved Brody. And he had loved them.

But now, God forgive him, but he could no less deny his feelings for Laney than he could stop his heart from beating or the sun from shining.

The way she was looking at him was more than he could handle, more than any man could handle, no matter what his strength. And Slade was definitely not a strong enough man to resist. His stomach fluttered and his legs trembled when she looked up at him that way. Her eyes were welcoming and her lips parted, practically begging to be kissed.

She closed the distance between them, and jumped into the gap his hesitance had created.

"I don't know whether or not you've heard the news, cowboy," she said in a rich, flirtatious tone that made him feel as if he was floating a good ten feet above the ground, "but *someone* put my name in the hat for me to be Serendipity's rodeo princess."

Her gaze playfully accused him and he gave his shoulders a light shrug.

"Always said you were a princess." His voice sounded terrible, high and squeaky, cracking as if he was a kid in the middle of puberty. He tried to smile but even that came out feeling awkward and cheesy.

It was one thing to be rid of his youthful foolishness, those character traits that had put him into a long string of difficulties of his own making. He had given little thought to the women he'd dated, making the best use of his charm and then walking away.

Now the tables were turned and he didn't like it one bit. Laney had turned him into a rambling idiot, made considerably worse by the meaningful smile she flashed him. She knew exactly what she was doing to his senses, and she clearly liked the power it gave her over him. She could lead him by the nose and he'd follow her anywhere.

"I'm perfectly aware of who threw my name into the hat, Prince Charming. Thanks a lot, by the way. I'm going to look like a moose out there on that truck. It would have been far better to leave the princessing to a young woman who could actually ride a horse."

"You," he disagreed, tapping the end of her nose, "will be absolutely beautiful out there. There's not a woman in Texas who could hope to hold a candle to you."

She actually appeared a little insecure at his heart-felt declaration, and suddenly he very much wanted to prove to her just how special she was. He'd gotten her into this situation in the first place, so it seemed only right that—

His thoughts vanished as he looked down at her and realized she'd tipped her chin upward and was standing very...very...close.

Waiting to be kissed?

He didn't know exactly how long he'd been waiting for this moment, but now he realized it was a lengthy time in coming. There had been so many barriers. Brody. The baby. The fact that she couldn't stand the sight of him when they'd first met. His own harsh feelings toward her. The way they'd tussled with each other.

Somehow, all of that had led up to this moment. Everything except Laney faded into the mist before him. Just him and this beautiful woman.

Just the two of them.

"Laney," he murmured huskily, running his fingers from her jaw to her chin, his thumbs brushing the soft stretch of skin on her cheekbones. "Princess. Look at me."

He wanted her to see who she was kissing, wanted her to know whose heart would never be the same after this moment.

When she looked at him, he knew beyond a doubt what she was seeing. She was seeing *him*, with all his vulnerabilities exposed, his strengths and weaknesses and mistakes and pain bared for her.

And love.

Her gaze reflected his, and as he bent his head and pressed his lips to hers, he could only thank God for giving him the opportunity to make his world right.

The taste of her lips, the peach flavor of her lip gloss, tugged his thoughts further from him, replacing them with all the emotions that up until now he'd been suppressing, not allowing himself to feel.

He slanted his head to deepen the kiss, then removed his hat and tossed it onto the dirt at his feet without a second thought, except that he needed to be as close to this woman as was humanly possible.

From now on he wouldn't let any barriers—physical or emotional— get in their way.

For as large and muscular a man as Slade was, his embrace was incredibly gentle. His touch was soft and his kiss was tender, both giving and taking, seeking the meaning of the moment and giving it.

This wasn't some young man taking what he wanted and leaving nothing in return. Slade was offering her his all.

And oh, how much she wanted to give him. So much she didn't know how to express—the way he'd stolen into her life as stealthily as a thief, not carrying off her heart but joining it to his.

Slade didn't try to push his advantage, though she knew full well that was how he would have acted in the past. Rather, he let her set the pace, letting her taste the depth of his emotion, only to draw back and make her chase for it.

She ran her hands down his powerful shoulders. Her fingers lingered over the strength and definition of his biceps. His arms quivered beneath her touch, and she wondered how difficult it was for him to rein in his emotions.

She knew how *she* felt—like a princess, glimmering and sparkling and galloping across an open field with the sun shining down on her.

She cupped his face in her hands, reveling in the scent of leather, the scratchy texture of his whiskers against her palms, the firm strength of his jaw and the myriad of feelings tumbling through her. Some were emotions she'd never thought to feel again, and others were brand-new to her.

He kissed her forehead and her cheeks and then bent his head, holding her close. His breath was heavy and he was shaking—or maybe she was the one quivering.

"Slade," she murmured, desperate to put words to the emotions she was experiencing. She stretched her consciousness to wrap her thoughts around the sounds in her mind but all she could seem to find was his name.

He murmured a guttural response that was not quite a word. It gave her a certain sense of satisfaction that their kiss had apparently left the same mark on Slade as it had on her, that he was as tongue-tied as she felt.

"Princess." He had more success with his words this time and he tightened his embrace around her.

Laney smiled into his chest, finally ready to hear what he had to tell her, how he felt about her. And then she could share all the beautiful emotions she felt for him. The future stretched before them, but they were no longer alone. They would figure it out between the two of them—the *three* of them.

"I pulled Night Terror." His words came out in an abrasive rush, pelting her with their sharp edges.

She gasped and pulled away from him. She'd opened

herself up to him, exposed her very heart to him, and he'd been doing—what?

Buttering her up so his news would slide down easier? Catching her on the easy side of what could arguably be one of the worst days of her life? The calm before the storm?

How *dare* he?

She chose anger over showing how hurt she felt, because anger kept her going while the pain she was experiencing might well cripple her.

He winced and ran a palm back over his hair, then reached for his hat, tapping the dust off of it before planting it firmly on his head, adjusting the brim low over electric blue eyes that were sparking fire.

"Why didn't you tell me?" she managed to choke out.

"I'm telling you now. I just found out a little while ago."

"But you thought it was perfectly acceptable to sneak in a kiss before laying that bolt from the blue on me, huh?

"Sneak? I wasn't—"

"I don't want to hear it, Slade." She didn't want to hear anything that passed through his deceitful lips. Her heart was ripping, one agonizing piece after another, and not only because he'd played her for a fool, stringing her along like the rest of his buckle bunnies.

No, it was because she was so incredibly angry with herself. She had completely fallen for his well-chorded tune, believed he was a changed man, one who could be depended on when the going got tough.

Someone she could fall in love with.

His jaw tightened and his gaze narrowed on her.

"Princess?" She found it ironic that his voice appeared laced with concern. He reached for her elbows as if to steady her.

She flinched inwardly, though outwardly she remained steady and unmoving. Her first impulse was to jerk her arms from his touch, which was gentle yet firm enough to keep her stable and upright. She resisted the compulsion and chose to stare him down instead. He could only hurt her if she let him, and she was too strong to let that happen.

When she got back home at the Becketts' ranch, locked securely in her own room, then she had no doubt she'd break down. But she'd hold herself together until then. She'd faced worse circumstances than the hulking cowboy looming over her with a semblance of worry lining his features.

Fool me once...

"You are as white as a sheet," he said, tilting his head to better meet her gaze. "You aren't going to pass out on me now, are you, princess?"

"Of course not," she snapped back. "And don't call me princess."

He pressed his lips together and shifted his gaze over her left shoulder.

"Um, excuse me" came a heavily accented Texan's voice from where Slade was looking. She glanced back to find Ian James, standing with his hat in his hands and shifting from one booted foot to another. His gaze was apologetic but his lips were quirking with amusement.

Great. Just great. Now she'd been caught behind the bleachers with a man whose reputation had to be as tarnished as old silver. To the uninformed observer, she and Slade would definitely appear to be in a compromising position.

She jerked out of Slade's grasp and turned to Ian. She tipped her chin and raised her brows, offering what she hoped was a confident smile.

"Sorry to interrupt, but Slade, the rodeo's about to start and the guys were wondering where you'd gotten off to."

"I'll be right there, Cap," Slade assured the man.

Ian nodded and briskly headed in the opposite direction without looking back. Laney had the impression he was trying to give them one last moment of privacy to finish what he probably took for a romantic interlude. How wrong could a man be? Other than the very great desire to wring his neck, Laney wanted nothing to do with Slade McKenna.

There was nothing left to say between them, and the sooner she got out of here and back to her seat, the better off she would be.

Yet no matter how angry she was with Slade, she couldn't put her worry aside over the danger he was about to face. Regardless of what had transpired between them or how negatively she viewed him now, she wasn't positive she could watch him ride Night Terror. The very thought made her stomach queasy.

She'd deal with it. She would *deal*. What other choice did she have?

"Laney —" Slade's hand snaked out to grab hers.

"We have nothing left to say to one another," she informed him without turning.

Rather than use his greater strength to turn her toward him, he slipped around her so they were face-to-face.

"Say the word," he said, his tone as sober as if he were taking a vow.

"Say *what*?"

"If you don't want me to ride Night Terror, I'll walk away from it."

Was he serious? He'd willingly give up something he'd been working on, maybe even dreamed about, ever since his best friend's death?

For her?

Part of her wanted to rail at him, tell him she didn't care one way or another whether he rode the stupid bull or not. Another part of her, the part ruled by a deep-seated longing for him that wouldn't go away, by emotions that confirmed that she harbored feelings that she didn't want to address, wanted to beg him to hang up his hat without riding.

But then his gaze met hers—those amazing, expressive blue eyes—and she saw that they were filled with longing. Pain. Compassion. And most of all, determination.

Suddenly she knew he would indeed walk away from his ride if she asked him to do it, and with just as much certainty, she realized she could not ask him to do so.

She had Brody's baby to honor Brody's life, cut short before he even knew he was going to be a father.

Slade only had this ride, this tribute to his friend, to the sport that had been such an important part of Brody's life.

For all Slade's faults, he had loved Brody and deserved this chance to honor his friend in the way he saw fit. She couldn't ask him to walk away from this now.

"No," she said before she lost her nerve.

"No, you don't want me to ride?" Disappointment flashed over his features but he quickly schooled them.

She shook her head. "No, I don't want you to give up

your ride because of me. Go ride Night Terror, Slade. You give that bull the what-for. Do it for Brody."

Slade adjusted the crown of his hat and jerked his chin to acknowledge her words. "For Brody."

He strode off without another glance in her direction. Maybe he thought she might change her mind if he looked back. Her throat closed around her hammering heart as she watched him turn the corner of the bleachers and disappear out of sight.

"Please, God, keep him safe."

Because she loved him.

It didn't matter what he'd done, or if he'd played fast and loose with her emotions. It didn't matter if his attention wandered elsewhere the moment his eight seconds were past, or even if he'd ever really cared for her at all.

The only thing that mattered right now was that he stayed safe. She would deal with what was or wasn't between them later.

The crowd had grown considerably and it was harder for her to make her way up the bleachers, but folks were very accommodating to her bulky, awkward frame, scooting out of the way to give her better footing. Many of the men even offered her a steadying hand on her way up to her seat between Carol and Jo.

"We were starting to wonder if Slade had carried you off," Carol teased.

Heat fused to Laney's cheekbones and it was all she could do to keep her face from crumpling.

"Oh, no," Jo said, tsking and shaking her head. "What is it, dear? You look terrible. Is it the baby?"

Laney shook her head and concentrated on calming her roiling stomach by focusing on Jo's self-made T-shirt. Love Me Some Texas Cowboys.

Yeah, not so much. Laney would prefer almost anything *but* that. As if she had any choice in the matter. The heart loved what the heart loved with no mind to what made any sense.

"The baby is fine," she managed to say. "It's Slade."

Grant and Frank leaned forward to join in the conversation.

"What about Slade?" Grant asked with a reassuring smile.

"He pulled Night Terror. I think that's what he wanted. He'd riding Brody's bull."

"Oh, my," Carol breathed, her face paling.

Instantly filled with remorse over the abrupt way she'd spilled the information about someone she knew the Becketts viewed as a second son, Laney reached for Carol's hands. "I'm so sorry. I was only thinking of myself. I can't imagine—" Tears sprang to her eyes and her sentence faded to silence.

"No. It's just as well I know now," Carol said, straightening her shoulders and offering a weak smile. "I knew it was Slade's wish for his last ride to be on Night Terror. I pray he bests that bull, for Brody's sake—and for his own."

"His own?" Laney repeated.

"Remember, Slade was there the night of Brody's accident. Maybe riding Night Terror will rid Slade of his own nightmares." Carol squeezed Laney's hands reassuringly. "It's time for all of us to move forward with our lives. That's what Brody would have wanted."

Carol gave her a knowing look that Laney didn't even try to misinterpret. Carol was completely aware that feelings were growing between her and Slade.

She hoped the Becketts wouldn't be too disappointed

to discover Slade was only passing through on his way to greener pastures.

The rodeo started and despite the anxiety hanging over her head, Laney found herself getting caught up in the excitement, the pageantry of roping and riding and barrels and bareback. She was glad she didn't have to report for her stint as rodeo princess until the very end, after the bull riding.

When Ian announced bull riding as the next event, Carol and Jo each took one of her hands. She was surrounded by love and support, and what woman could ask for more? The Becketts were her family now, and Jo like a beloved aunt.

"He's been riding bulls since he was knee high to a grasshopper," Frank assured her in the scratchy voice of an older man. "He'll be fine, Laney. Mark my words."

Her heart in her throat, she observed the first three bull riders take their turns. It was crazy scary stuff, with the bulls kicking and turning every which way, a completely different experience than watching the bucking broncs. Two of the three cowboys couldn't keep their seats for more than a couple of seconds, and getting themselves off the bulls appeared every bit as dangerous as the rides themselves.

And Slade wasn't riding just any bull. He was riding Night Terror.

She strained to see him over the top of the bullpens and finally spotted him as he crawled over the gate to get situated on Night Terror. Already, the pen was shaking from the unpredictable movements of the animal within.

She couldn't catch a breath as she watched him, but neither could she look away. Even at a distance she could see the tension rippling over his neck and shoulders and the intensity of his expression. He made a magnificent picture astride the bull, a cowboy among cowboys as he made last minute adjustments to his seat and his grip.

He was all man. All cowboy. No wonder he had women falling at his feet.

Then he nodded and the gate opened.

Laney wanted to cover her eyes but she simply couldn't look away.

Night Terror lived up to his name. She'd never seen such a ferocious beast. The bull was determined to shake Slade off his back. Night Terror threw his head and his back feet simultaneously, turned first one way and then the other without letting up, planting all four feet at once and then leaping into the air, bucking wildly.

Slade somehow adjusted to every movement like the trained athlete he was. Laney was marking the seconds with the beating of her heart, but still the buzzer failed to ring.

Surely it had been eight seconds. Where was the buzzer?

Suddenly Night Terror turned and charged at the wall.

Time stopped. Laney's prayers intensified, though she hardly knew she was praying at all. There was only Slade and Night Terror, locked in a deadly dance.

The bull turned at the last second, just before slamming Slade into the wall. Night Terror appeared to recover just a hairbreadth before Slade could completely recover his balance, and shot for the wall a second time. The two bullfighters in the arena were trying to prevent that from happening, but the bull seemed unaware of the horses or the hollering, hat-waving cowboys. His only intent appeared to be getting Slade off his back any way he could.

Laney stood, crying out for Slade. The crowd rose also, screaming their approval of Slade's ride.

The buzzer.

It had sounded, hadn't it? Just before Night Terror had charged the wall that second time? Or was Laney just so desperate to have Slade safe that she'd imagined it?

But no. Laney breathed a sigh of relief as Slade accepted the assistance of one of the bullfighters to get himself off the bull, then jogged over to retrieve his hat, which he'd lost during the first jarring second of the ride.

He waved his hat in the air to acknowledge the roaring crowd, then settled it on his head, found Laney's gaze and tipped his hat to her.

Prince Charming.

His dedication reminded her of all those stories she'd read of knights winning their jousting matches in order to win their lady's favor.

He'd just acknowledged her in front of everyone. They'd been seen together enough throughout the past few weeks that she doubted anyone would doubt his intentions.

His princess.

Princess. She'd completely forgotten that she was supposed to meet the production team behind the stable so they could parade her around the arena in the back of a pickup truck.

Serendipity's rodeo princess.

Slade's princess.

No matter how much she denied it, that was what really mattered.

She scrambled down from the bleachers as fast as she could in her condition, with more *excuse me's* and *pardon me's* than she cared to count.

She rounded the end of the bleachers at a full-out jog and ran smack-dab into the middle of a broad chest. The heartening scent of leather and cowboy assaulted her. The arms that snaked around her waist were familiar and reassuring.

Slade.

She hugged him tight and he chuckled. "Good to see you, too. Goin' somewhere, princess?"

"You did it!" She hugged him even harder, not wanting to let him go even for a moment. Never mind that earlier she'd completely written him off—or at least thought he was done with her. "You rode Night Terror."

"Of course I did," he responded with that confident, jaunty smile that made her insides melt. It was so— *Slade.* "Was there ever any doubt?"

"No. Yes. I'm just glad you're safe."

"That makes two of us," he agreed, then slid his hands up to her shoulders and pointed her in the direction of the arena's entrance. "Now if I don't miss my guess, there are some folks waiting for your pretty face and sparkling personality to make your Serendipity debut."

Instead of letting her go, he slid a familiar, comfortable arm around her shoulders and walked with her, even extending his assistance to sweeping her off her feet and depositing her in the back of the truck.

"Have a care, princess. Don't fall off."

She wrinkled her nose at him, then held her hand out to him just as the truck started moving away.

"I'm proud of you," she whispered as their fingers slid apart. "And so is Brody."

Chapter Eleven

Laney was proud of him.

The dark, thunderous cloud in his chest that had been with him since Brody's death had lifted when he'd heard the eight second buzzer, but Laney's words swirled around his insides like soft ribbons, lighting up the void where previously only the darkness of grief had lurked.

He shook his head and jogged to the corner of the arena where he could watch the crowd's enthusiastic reception of the woman he loved. He had no doubt that they would feel the same way as he did about her. Just as they would welcome Brody's baby when the time came. The kid would have more honorary aunts and uncles than the poor little person would be able to count.

Slade was glad he'd made the ride on Night Terror today, but he wasn't the least bit sorry that it would be his last. The eight seconds—they hadn't mattered. Not compared to the sweet moments before the ride when he'd held Laney in his arms.

Now *that* was when everything had been set right in his world.

Only somehow it had gone all wrong. He couldn't forget that part of it. He still didn't know what had happened, only that he'd managed to make a mess out of it and needed to make things right with her.

He would do that—once he figured out exactly what it was he'd done, which would be the second she got finished with this stint as Serendipity's rodeo princess. He would whisk her away someplace private, apologize right out of the gate, and let her tell him where he'd gone wrong after they'd made up. But first, he wanted her to enjoy every moment of her time in the spotlight. No woman had ever deserved it more, and he was proud of her.

The large red truck slowly circled the arena once, and then twice. Laney had one hand braced on the hood to stabilize her and was waving to the roaring crowd with the other. Her smile said it all.

He grinned, enjoying the sight of her bright eyes and happy face.

The vehicle turned to do one last loop around the arena in an unrehearsed encore in response to her popularity. Slade was opening the gate that would allow the truck to exit the arena when suddenly Laney dropped out of sight inside the bed of the truck.

Slade's stomach took a leaden plunge at the same moment his heart jammed into his throat as panic struck through him.

Had the truck hit something in the arena? Had she somehow lost her balance and fallen down?

Lord, take care of Laney and the baby.

Slade didn't wait to see if she'd get back on her feet. He was over the fence so fast he wasn't even sure whether he'd scaled it or flown over it, but the second his boots hit the dirt he was running toward her with every ounce of power his body possessed.

What if she had fainted? Hit her head?

What if something was wrong with the baby?

He reached the truck and grabbed the side with one hand, flinging his feet over the rim in one smooth move and scrambling toward the woman he loved.

He was supposed to protect her. What if something was seriously wrong with her? He'd never felt so helpless in his life. Not knowing what else to do, he sent another prayer heavenward.

God had this.

He was relieved to see that Laney was conscious, but she was slumped with her back resting against the wall of the truck with her elbows resting on her knees. Her face was hidden in her palms so he couldn't see her expression.

"Princess?" Slade asked, scrambling to her side, crouching beside her and gently embracing her shoulders, careful not to move her. "What happened, honey? Are you okay? And the baby? Is something wrong with the baby?" He realized he was shooting off questions like a semiautomatic pistol.

Pop. Pop. Pop.

Just exactly what she didn't need right now.

He winced and she raised her head. Her eyes were full of unshed tears, her breath was coming in short gasps followed by short hiccups. Most alarming of all, her face was flushed to a cherry red. Beads of sweat dotted her forehead and her lips were quivering.

If he didn't know any better, he'd think she was suffering from a high fever. But they'd been together only minutes before and she'd been fine. She hadn't looked or acted ill—far from it. He brushed a hand across her cheek just to be certain. If anything, her skin felt cold and clammy, completely at odds with the color of her face.

He knocked on the window of the truck and gestured for the driver to leave the arena. As far as he was concerned, Laney's sudden drop into the truck bed was already a spectacle enough and he wanted to get her out of the public eye so he could find out what was really wrong with her.

The truck driver took it slow and easy, and Slade held Laney tight against any unexpected bumps along the way. He knew Delia was somewhere in the crowd, as well as Serendipity's paramedics Ben and Zach. He had every expectation that at least one of them, hopefully all three, would have seen Laney's fall and would even now be on their way to assist her.

Until then, there was no one to help her but Slade, who had very little medical training other than the first aid certification he'd had to have to become a small-town policeman. He regretted that he hadn't paid much attention in that class, only enough to pass the test and get by with. He desperately wished he'd taken it seriously—but back then, he hadn't taken much of anything seriously.

"Do you want to lie down?" he asked gently grasping her hand in his. She was quivering and he gave her a reassuring squeeze. "I'm sure Delia is on her way, but in the meantime, won't you tell me how I can make you more comfortable. Are you having contractions?"

That seemed like the most likely scenario so he was surprised when she shook her head. The color in her cheeks darkened even further.

"Princess, talk to me."

He ticked down the probabilities in his mind. She didn't want to lie down. She wasn't having contractions. She was flushed but not feverish. Yet something was clearly wrong, something that had caused her to collapse.

"Did you lose your balance?" he guessed, racking his brain for any other possible explanations. "Did the truck hit a rut and send you sprawling?"

He wanted to kick himself. He'd been the one to suggest the whole "back of the truck" idea. He should have known that in her condition it would be difficult for her to maintain her balance. He should have considered something safer, like riding inside the truck, or rigging up a seat for her to safely sit in. Or even better, personally escorting her while she walked.

Anything, except what he'd done.

A single tear escaped her eyes and trailed down her cheek and Slade brushed it away with the pad of his thumb. He regarded her closely for a moment, his gaze briefly catching hers, but she quickly turned her head away.

He continued to consider and then discard one possible scenario after the other. Her eyes were bright with unshed tears and yet she didn't appear to be in any kind of physical pain. No contractions, and he mentally drew a line through twisting an ankle when she nixed his idea that she might have lost her balance.

He had nothing.

"Princess, talk to me," he begged again.

She groaned and still refused to look at him. "I have never been so embarrassed in all my life!"

Embarrassed?

Here he was thinking she was injured or that something was wrong with Baby Beckett and she was *embarrassed*?

"Of what? I don't understand. Because you were the center of attention for a cheering crowd of spectators? Surely you knew what you were getting into when you agreed to be the rodeo princess. The last rodeo you did was bigger than this one." He was rambling, spitting out all the thoughts that were tumbling through him, and he pressed his lips together to stem the flow of words.

"Is Delia on her way, do you think?" She flashed him a furtive glance before returning her gaze to—anyplace except for his face.

"I thought you said you weren't injured," he said, his concern for her flaring once again in his chest. Her voice did sound a little weak.

She made an indecipherable sound from deep in her throat.

"I'm not injured, Slade. I—my—"

"What?" His emotions had been stretched as far as they could go. He couldn't help her if he didn't know what was wrong. He knew there was much to work out between them, but did she not trust him enough to tell him what had happened to her?

She scrubbed her palms down her red-stained cheeks. "My water broke."

"Your—your *what*?" He barely resisted the urge to scramble backward to see if there was indeed a puddle of fluid around her, but he restrained himself, knowing such an action would further humiliate her.

"Okay," he said, giving her shoulder an awkward pat. This was so far out of his comfort zone it wasn't even funny. What did a man say to a statement like that? "Um—well, that's normal, isn't it?"

Where was Delia?

He'd even take Zach or Ben right now, although he suspected Laney would much prefer the woman doctor to either of the two male paramedics.

"Normal, maybe, but not in front an entire stadium full of people." She groaned deeply. "I can't believe this is happening."

He wanted to reassure her in some way. It was happening. *It* was happening. She was about to have Brody's baby, and sooner rather than later.

Where was Delia?

And what was he supposed to do with Laney? He now understood why she didn't want to move, and especially why she didn't want to lie down, but somehow he had to get her out of here, transport her to the hospital where she'd planned on giving birth.

"Hey, Laney," said Delia, climbing over the tailgate. "Sorry it took me so long. I was clear at the top of one of the bleachers and it took me a moment to make my way through the crowd. What's happening, hon?"

Slade almost slumped in relief. The reinforcements had finally arrived—or rather, the main troops, since he was less than useless in this situation. Definitely more of a hamper than a help.

Or worse.

His gut twisted as a new thought entered his mind. Laney had been just fine before the rodeo—before he'd ridden Night Terror.

What if he was responsible for her water breaking? What if she was in labor because of the stress he'd put on her by having to watch him ride the bull that had killed Brody?

He squeezed her hand tightly in a silent apology. If he could go back and do it again, he'd—

What? Pay more attention to the signs? *Were* there signs? If there were, he'd completely missed them.

Laney and Delia were speaking to each other in low tones, but Slade picked up the words *labor* and *hospital* out of the conversation.

"Does she need an ambulance?" he asked, anxiety piercing every nerve ending in his body. "Can I ride with her?"

Delia's brow rose at his request and she chuckled.

"Don't worry, Slade. She's not going to have Baby Beckett in the back of this truck, or even within the next hour. She may not even start having contractions by then. It could be days yet, but we need to get her checked out. That said, we have plenty of time to get her to the hospital in San Antonio. You have your birth plan registered at Mercy Medical Center, right Laney?"

Laney nodded.

"We should get going then," Slade affirmed, and both women turned their surprised gazes upon him. His own gaze widened and he shrugged. "What?"

"We?" Delia asked with a chuckle.

"Well, yeah. If you think I'm going to stay back here in town while Laney goes through labor and delivery all by herself, you have another thing coming."

Laney's face had lost some of its color after Delia had arrived, but now her blush returned in spades.

"What?" Slade asked again.

"You can't—that is, Carol is my birth partner. She'll

be the one giving me support during the delivery," Laney explained.

Now it was Slade's turn to color as heat rose from his boots to his hat. He shook his head vehemently. "No, I didn't mean—no way. I'll be the one pacing outside the door to the room waiting to hand out cigars."

Laney wrinkled her nose. "Cigars?"

It was a moderately warm day in Texas. How had it suddenly gotten so hot out here? And where had all the oxygen disappeared to? He felt as if he was choking. He leaned back on his heels and took off his hat, wiping his suddenly wet brow and tunneling his fingers back through his hair.

"It's only an expression," he assured her as he stood. "I'm not going to contribute to anyone's vices. But I need to be there at the hospital. Please."

He shifted uncomfortably, suddenly feeling like a complete outsider, trying to push his nose where it didn't belong. Why did he think he had any right to accompany her to the hospital? He wasn't family. And at the moment, he wasn't certain he and Laney were even friends.

Delia looked at Laney with an enquiring smile. "Your call, hon."

"Yes, of course I want Slade to be there."

He let out his breath in an audible huff of air, relief flooding through him. He'd be there when Brody's baby—and *Laney's* baby—was born.

Carol and Grant reached the truck about the same time Ben and Zach got there, followed immediately by Jo and Frank. Everyone else who'd gathered for the rodeo seemed to be giving them a wide berth, respecting their privacy, and perhaps wondering if they'd need to make a quick exit—which in Slade's opinion, they did. Delia updated everyone without embarrassing Laney with every last detail. She assured Ben and Zach that an ambulance wasn't necessary and they quickly made their excuses.

"We'll be taking her over to the hospital," Grant informed everyone. "We're all set. She has a suitcase packed and in the trunk, so we're good to go."

He hadn't realized Laney had prepared in advance. She even had her suitcase packed for her stay in the hospital.

But it wasn't yet her due date. She had at least a few days left, didn't she?

"You're sure she doesn't need any extra help?" Slade protested. It wasn't that he doubted Delia's word, exactly. She was the doctor. But he couldn't help but be worried about Laney. "What if she starts her contractions? What if she needs pain medicine? Shouldn't she be transferred by ambulance, just in case?"

Laney reached for his hand. "I'll be fine. I'm having a natural birth."

"What does that mean?" He looked from Laney to Delia and back again, his throat tightening. He was certain he wasn't going to like whatever he was about to hear.

"She's not going to be medicated during the birth," Carol inserted.

"What?" Slade repeated. "Why would she do that?"

He didn't know what labor felt like, but he knew how Laney had looked when she'd last experienced contractions—and those were *fake* ones. He couldn't imagine why she'd want to subject herself to the real thing. Besides, it wasn't the dark ages. Why endure pain when it wasn't a necessity?

"It's too complicated to get into right now," Laney informed him. "In case you've forgotten, I need to get to the hospital, probably sooner rather than later."

Slade pressed his hat back on his head and reached for her other hand. She blushed. "How do I—er—"

He realized she was talking about her water breaking. She didn't want to stand up, probably especially in mixed company. But she was going to have to move if she was going to get transferred to Grant's car. He'd gone to bring the car around and Frank had likewise gone to get his truck, so he was the only man left in the area. He hoped she knew she could depend on him, no matter what. He might be freaking out a little bit on the inside, but on the outside, he was going to be her rock.

"No need to worry about it, princess. Everyone here loves you."

He knew every eye turned on him but he didn't care. His only concern was the woman he was carefully assisting to her feet. As soon as she was standing, he wrapped one arm around her waist and held her hand to steady her. He didn't look anywhere except her face.

"Take it easy, princess. One step at a time."

"I can walk," she responded. "I'm not sick, just embarrassed. You don't have to hover over me."

He begged to differ but decided against saying so out loud. Instead, he hopped off the tail gate and swept her into his arms, carrying her to Grant and Carol's vehicle. She protested, but Slade would have none of it. He didn't care if her jeans were soaked. The only thing that mattered to him was that Laney was properly cared for.

As he gently deposited her in her seat, she reached for his hand.

"Thank you," she whispered, her voice coarse.

His brow rose and despite his anxiety over the situation, he gave her his best confident grin, hoping it looked reassuring from the outside, because inside he was shaking. "No problem."

He thought she was talking about him carrying her to the car, but she adamantly shook her head. "Not for this. For everything. For—"

Grant broke in, reminding them that they needed to go. Everyone gathered wished Laney well and expressed their excitement of seeing Baby Beckett soon.

"I'll meet you at the hospital," Delia assured Laney, then tapped on the top of the car to let Grant know he could take off.

Slade wanted to ask them to wait. He needed to hear what Laney had been about to say. What did she mean, that she was thankful for *everything*?

But the moment had passed and Grant pulled his car from the arena drive. He clenched his hands into nervous fists, Slade watched until the vehicle was out of sight. He felt oddly lost and empty.

He didn't know what she'd meant, but he knew what was in his heart. He, too, was thankful for everything he'd found with her. Now was not the time, but he hoped soon he would be able to show her just how grateful he was.

Right now, all he could do was drive to the hospital— and pray as he'd never done before.

Laney's contractions started about halfway to the hospital in San Antonio. To her surprise, they weren't nearly as strong as the Braxton Hicks contractions she'd experience a few weeks earlier. Not only were they shorter and less intense, but further apart, so much so that she'd wondered if she really should be going to the hospital so soon.

Carol had gently reminded her that it was an important part of her birth plan, because the hospital had instructed her to come in right away if her water broke or contractions started coming at seven minutes apart since she had so far to drive to get there.

She didn't know how Slade managed to catch up with the Becketts' car, since it would have been impossible for him to have left until at least a few minutes after they had, but twenty minutes into their drive, Laney looked back to find Slade's truck right behind them. She hoped he hadn't broken the speed limit too much in order to catch up with them.

She found a great deal of amusement and distraction watching him.

Poor Slade. He might have felt better had he simply accompanied them in the Becketts' car, but she didn't want him getting stuck in San Antonio with no way to go get a meal for himself or to return home after Baby Beckett was born. Not to mention the fact that he would no doubt have hovered over her and made a bigger deal out of her labor than it really was at this point.

He didn't exactly tailgate, but he kept only a short distance between his truck and the Becketts' car. From her position in the backseat, she could easily see him through the rear window. His hat was, as usual when he was under stress, pulled down low over his brow, so she wasn't able to see his eyes, but she knew him well enough to know he was edgy. He drove with both hands clenching the wheel and his whole upper body hunched over the steering wheel, as tense as a wildcat ready to spring on its prey.

He tailed them into San Antonio, but at some point he lost them, maybe getting caught in the congested traffic. Laney didn't have time to worry about it because they arrived at the hospital and she was whisked up to the triage room on the delivery floor. From there, she was transferred into a large, comfortable birthing room, where Carol and Jo stayed with her, offering good company and distraction to keep her from getting too anxious about the whole process.

It was several hours before the contractions became regular and painful, but once she crested the first hill, her labor accelerated into full speed ahead. Eventually Carol stepped out for a moment, presumably to let Grant and Frank know how things were going— and Slade, of course, who probably needed the update more than anyone.

Carol came back and reported that he had, indeed, found the hospital and had been admitted to the ward with the special code Grant had texted him. Word had it that Grant and Frank, both experienced in the unpredictability of childbirth, had each grabbed a cup of coffee and were playing cards outside the room. Slade, on the other hand, was apparently prowling right outside the door. Carol laughingly said she wasn't certain his hat would make it through the process.

Laney remembered how nervous he'd been the day he'd first taken her to see Delia. He'd been lumbering around then, too. She hoped the waiting room here at the hospital gave him a little bit more room to stretch, because she had the feeling he was in for a long night.

After that everything became fuzzy as the contractions started coming one after another in rapid succession. She pulled inside herself, concentrating on her birth coaches and the breathing she'd been taught to use.

Baby Beckett arrived just after half past two in the morning. During the delivery Laney was in so much pain she couldn't think beyond the last contraction, but the moment she heard the baby's cry, her pain was forgotten.

Carol pressed a hand to her sweaty forehead and brushed her hair back with her palm. "It's a boy, honey. You have a son."

"Can I— Is he healthy?"

"They're cleaning him up right now, dear. Isn't this exciting? Your baby is here! Ten fingers and ten toes," Jo assured her.

Laney was incredibly tired, but joy filled her heart so full she thought it would burst when the nurse placed her baby in her arms. She was so choked up she wasn't sure she could speak, but she managed one word.

"Slade."

"I'll go get him now, honey," Carol assured her. "I'm sure all the men are anxious to see this little one, but I have no doubt that Slade is the most eager of the three of them.

She stared down at the tiny child in her arms and breathed a prayer of thanksgiving. The baby had a thatch of thick brown hair on top of his head and the clearest, bluest eyes she'd ever seen.

Brody's eyes.

Slade was the first into the room but not the first one to her bedside. He hung back, hat in hand, shifting from one booted foot to the other while the older men came forward and took turns congratulating her on the baby's birth, giving all of the expected ooh's and aah's in all the right places.

"All right, you two," Jo said, rounding up Frank and Grant. "Why don't we go get something from the cafeteria. I'm starving."

"Cafeteria's closed," Frank said with a shake of his head. "It's nearly three in the morning."

The look Jo gave Frank made Laney chuckle. Jo's eyes widened and she jerked her head toward Slade. "Then we'll find a vending machine."

"Oh," Frank said, his voice gruff. "You want to give Slade and Laney some time alone. Why didn't you just say that in the first place, woman?"

Jo sighed and rolled her eyes. "See what I have to put up with? Grant and Carol, would you like anything from the *vending machine*?" She gave the last couple of words enough extra emphasis to get a grunt out of Frank.

"We'll join you," Carol said, and Grant nodded.

"We'll be back to check on you soon, dear," Jo said, patting Laney's hand. "Congratulations again on bringing that sweet little one into this world. He's so beautiful. You've done Brody proud."

Tears sprang to Laney's eyes, but they were tears of joy.

Slade tentatively approached her bedside. His face was lined with concern but his eyes glittered with excitement.

"Hey, princess," he whispered with all the reverence of someone in the middle of a church service. He rolled the brim of his hat in his fists. "You're okay?"

Laney chuckled. "I'm better than okay. I've never been happier."

He leaned forward and tilted his head so he could get a better look at the baby.

"It's a boy?" His face was full of such wonder it was almost as if he'd never seen a newborn baby before.

She nodded and adjusted her son so Slade could get a better look at him.

"Slade," she said with a soft smile, first at her baby and then at the man standing respectfully at her side. "Meet Brody Beckett."

Chapter Twelve

Brody Beckett.

Slade was in awe. Laney had delivered a son, and he was as beautiful and perfect as his parents. He couldn't swallow around the lump of emotion in his throat and his heart was beating so fast he was certain Laney must be able to hear it.

"He's beautiful," Slade whispered, running his palm across the baby's forehead, then lifting his hand to brush the back of his fingers against Laney's soft cheek. Her hair was sticking to her temples and she looked as if she'd run a marathon, but to Slade she had never looked better. "And you, too, princess."

"Well, I'll take the compliment on Baby Brody's behalf, but if you are going to stand there and tell me I look good I'm going to send you away for fibbing."

Slade crossed his index finger over his heart. "I mean it. I do."

As he'd paced out in front of the birthing room for hours on end waiting for the baby's birth, he'd gone back and forth between worrying about Laney and rehearsing what he was going to say to her when he saw her. But the moment he'd seen Laney with Baby Brody tucked safely in her arms, his mind went blank. He'd been mortified when Jo had suggested he needed to be alone with Laney—as if they were a couple.

A man could dream. He could plan. But the moment he'd stepped into the room and had seen the glowing new mother with her baby, a whole new set of emotions had overtaken him, feelings he'd never before experienced.

He wasn't sure his heart could take it, just looking at her soft smile and tender gaze. He'd been thinking of a thousand ways to approach the subject of her future, but now there were no words. He wasn't worthy of this woman or little Brody. They deserved so much more than he could give them.

Laney shifted to one side of the bed and patted the space beside her. "Sit here for a second."

He'd never felt so awkward in his life as he perched clumsily where she had indicated. "Okay, but only for a moment. You need to spend some time alone with Baby Brody. And I'm sure you need your rest."

"Well, that much is true. I am exhausted, but I'm glad you're here."

"You are?"

"You don't have to sound so surprised. You've supported me through everything the last couple of months. Of course I want you here."

He shook his head. He'd done everything *except* support her. Had she so quickly forgotten how big of a jerk he'd been when she'd first come to Serendipity?

"Would you like to hold little Brody?"

"Me? I—" Slade hedged. He'd never actually held a

newborn and had no idea what he was doing. He didn't want to accidentally hurt the little guy.

Laney adjusted his arm and held the baby out to him, showing him how to cradle the baby's neck in his hand.

Slade was quivering inside and he wondered if Laney could see the way he was shaking. He stared down at the infant for a long moment, in complete awe of the little one. The curl of his ears, his button of a nose, the way he sucked noisily on his fist. But most of all, Slade was struck by his bright blue eyes, unfocused but nonetheless intent on Slade's face.

"He has Brody's eyes," Laney said, as if she'd read his mind.

He nodded and swallowed hard. "And your hair."

She chuckled. "Yes, I suppose he does."

"Brody would be proud," he murmured.

When he glanced up at her he found her big brown eyes were full of tears and her lips were quivering.

"Hey, I'm sorry, princess. I didn't mean to make you cry. Not today, of all days."

She blinked back her tears but her smile was wide and genuine. "I'm not sad, Slade. These are tears of joy. I know Brody would be proud of his son."

"Yes, he would," Slade said in a high, singsong voice he'd never before used in his life but seemed oddly appropriate now. "Yes, he would. Your daddy would be so proud of you, little one. So proud."

He kissed the baby's cheek, marveling at how soft it was and how sweet little Brody smelled. Brand-new.

"You're probably tickling his cheek with your whiskers," Laney said with a laugh, brushing her hand over the baby's head and then settling it on Slade's jaw.

"Oh," he said, drawing back. "Sorry."

"Would you stop apologizing for every little thing? Your scruff is fine. In fact, I like you that way."

She liked him that way? He didn't know whether that was a good thing or a bad thing. Was she saying she found him attractive, or just making a passing comment about his beard? He needed to know but didn't know how to ask. Instead, he spoke to the baby.

"So, little man, your mama and your uncle Slade are going to teach you everything you need to know to grow up on a ranch. And I'm going to teach you how to throw and catch a ball, and ride a horse, and rope a calf, and—"

"Don't you think you ought to let him grow up a little bit before you start throwing balls at him?"

He grinned and winked at her. "I can wait. I'll always be there for him."

And you.

Why couldn't he say the words? Why was he so tongue-tied all of the sudden? He was the one who usually blurted stuff out without thinking. Now he'd done all the thinking and he couldn't seem to say the words.

He took extra care transferring Baby Brody back into the crook of Laney's arm. She was simply stunning as she gazed down at the swaddled infant. It was no wonder he had no words. Her beauty left him speechless.

He'd rehearsed this moment a million times as he paced the waiting room. He had a ring burning a hole in the pocket of his jeans. He'd made a little detour once he'd hit San Antonio to visit a jewelry store, with every intention in the world of proposing to her. And now his mouth couldn't seem to form the words. What a time to lose his composure.

He cleared his throat and reached deep inside himself

for the confidence that seemed to have deserted him, maybe because this was the most important moment of his life, the fork in the road that would change his path. Only instead of him being the one who'd choose the direction he would take, it was all up to Laney.

His princess.

Laney wasn't sure what was running through Slade's mind and she wasn't certain she wanted to know. He was acting squirrely. For a moment he'd looked as if he was ready to speak, and the next thing she knew he'd risen to his feet and lumbered over to the window, where he stood silently gazing outside.

Uncle Slade, he'd called himself. Baby Brody's honorary uncle. Was that how he thought of himself? Because that wasn't how she saw him at all.

As far as the Becketts were concerned, he was almost family, but to her he was so much more. She'd learned to depend on his strength and the way he chose a course and then stayed on it. He didn't just think about how to solve problems—he did everything in his power to fix them, even if he was a little overbearing at times. It was all from the goodness of his heart, and she needed his presence in her life.

She missed him when he wasn't with her—his amazing blue eyes, the way one corner of his lips kicked up when he was amused by something, even the way he always pulled his cowboy hat low over his brow when he didn't want anyone else to see what he was thinking.

She loved everything about him. She loved *him*.

But he'd just as much as come out with the fact that he considered himself an honorary uncle to her son. And perhaps that was what it had always been about—

being a part of little Brody's life, protecting him and watching out for him.

Her heart ached at the thought of seeing Slade around the Becketts as her son grew up, with him but not really *with* him. She couldn't imagine living that way, just as she could no longer imagine her life with Slade not in it.

If there was one thing she'd learned through her hasty marriage, her separation and Brody's accidental death, it was that nothing in life was certain. There were no promises of tomorrow. Every day was a gift from God and not to be taken lightly, but lived to the fullest.

Loved to the fullest.

Slade might not want to hear what she was about to say. He might be surprised—shocked even. She was going to astonish herself if she was able to get the words out of her mouth and her feelings out in the open. She didn't have the faintest idea how to start or what to say, she only knew that she had to expose her heart to him before he walked out of this room believing he was nothing more than Baby Brody's *Uncle Slade*.

He turned from the window just as she began to speak.

"I think you—" she started, but she couldn't seem to raise her voice above a whisper and he didn't hear her.

"There's not much of a view out there," he said at the same time. He turned to her and shoved his hands into the front pockets of his jeans. "You can't even see any trees or anything. Just the side of another building."

Her mouth shut. She had no idea how to respond to that.

"I've been thinking," he continued, and Laney's heart clenched. He resumed his seat next to her but she couldn't read his gaze. He leaned one arm over her legs and smiled down at the baby. "I feel like I need to apologize."

"Again?"

This isn't where she wanted the conversation to go and she was stymied by it. Could the man just not stop saying he was sorry? Or maybe say it once as a generic statement that would cover all past and future apologies?

"Yes, again." He shrugged and his gaze met hers.

"What is it this time?"

"I had a lot of time to think while I was waiting for Baby Brody to be born. I have a question to ask you and I want you to be honest me." His tone was even and his expression unreadable, but she thought she caught a glimpse of something in his eyes.

Her breath caught and held. Was he—could he feel as she felt, was his heart already entwined with hers?

"Was it because of me that your water broke?"

She let out her breath in a rush. Of all the things she expected—or hoped—he would say, that was not even in the ballpark.

"How on earth could you imagine my water breaking had anything to do with you?"

He shrugged, looking miserable. He shifted his gaze to the baby. "It happened right after I rode Night Terror. Your due date isn't for a few days yet. I thought maybe the stress of seeing me on that bull might have put you over the top, er —sent you into labor."

She sputtered out a laugh. One thing was for certain— if she was blessed with a life with Slade McKenna, it would never be boring.

"I hate to be the one to inform you of this," she said with a wry smile, "but the world does not revolve around you. My water broke because it was time for Baby Brody to make his grand entrance. It had absolutely nothing to do with you whatsoever. It was God's perfect timing and nothing to do with me watching a stubborn cowboy ride a bull in his best friend's honor."

"Oh." He sounded deflated. "I'm glad."

"Did you *want* to be the cause of the baby's birth?"

He stood abruptly. "No. No! I was terrified that I'd made a terrible mistake and that my foolishness might have put you and the baby in danger."

"Well, you can put that thought aside and rest easy, although I could very happily never hear another word about bull riding as long as I live."

"I'll try, princess, but that might be difficult, seeing as there's a rodeo in Serendipity every year and I'm a retired bull rider." He flashed a wink and a smile, turning all the charm he had on her and making her heart flip over.

She was long past believing she was immune to him.

"It all turned out exactly the way it was supposed to be," he continued.

Not *exactly*. Not the way she really wanted it to be.

She was about to put her entire future, her son's future and her very heart on the line, but it had to be done. She could no longer stay silent. She had to know—and so did he.

And if he brushed her off, at least he would know how she felt. It might be awkward for a while afterward when *Uncle Slade* came to see the baby, but they'd get past it eventually, or at least he would. She might never recover.

She took a deep breath and plunged in with no idea

whether she was going to sink or swim. "About that title of yours..."

He raised a brow. "What title? I didn't win anything. One of the younger fellows beat my score."

Despite the tension rippling through her, she had to laugh. She was ready to make a declaration of her everlasting love and he was thinking about the rodeo title he hadn't won. As if he didn't already have enough enormous silver belt buckles in his wardrobe.

"I wasn't talking about the rodeo."

He shook his head. "Then, what?"

"Uncle Slade. I'm not sure that's the right thing for Baby Brody to call you."

He blanched and turned away from her, striding toward the window, and she realized what she'd meant to say and what had actually come out of her mouth were two different things entirely, and she'd unintentionally hurt the man she loved.

"I'm sorry," she said, her throat tightening around the words. "This time it's me who needs to apologize.

He tossed a glance over his shoulder. "For what?"

She started to tell him but he interrupted.

"No, you're right. I overstepped when I called myself Baby Brody's uncle. I'm not family. Not really."

"But I'd like you to be."

He pivoted on the soles of his boots and swept his hat off his head in one smooth move. He was at her bedside only moments later, and for once he wasn't masking his emotions. She could see it all—hope, trepidation and—

He sat down next to her with one hand on the baby and the other against her cheek. She struggled to contain the tears that burned at the back of her eyes, knowing that crying would ruin everything. Slade always stepped up to deal with any problem, and he would definitely see tears as a problem. He wouldn't see them as the happy tears they were, and she didn't want to take the time to explain it to him. Her heart was too full, ready to explode if they didn't get on with it.

"There is nothing I want more than to be in your life. In Baby Brody's life. But you're right. I don't want to be Uncle Slade. I would—" He paused and jammed his hand into the pocket of his jeans. "I'm doing this all wrong. I got you a ring. I had this whole speech planned, and then somehow the conversation went in a different direction and I didn't know what to say, and now—"

It was time to break in before Slade ran out of breath and passed out on her, because he certainly didn't look as if his declaration was going to end any time soon. She rarely heard the strong, silent cowboy say so many words in a day, much less in one long string that sounded like a single sentence.

"Yes."

He continued as if he didn't hear her. "I know I can be stubborn sometimes, and we've had more than our share of tussles, but I promise—" He paused, looking as if someone had shaken him awake from a deep sleep. "Wait—what? Did you just say *yes*?"

"Yes."

"Yes, you'll marry me?" He sounded astounded, as if he hadn't known what her response would be until he'd heard it. How could he not have known?

She shifted Baby Brody to her right and held out her left hand. "Yes, I'll marry you. In fact, if you hadn't gotten to it soon, I was going to ask you."

"You were?" He still looked stunned, but he had the

presence of mind to slide the diamond solitaire onto her finger.

"It's beautiful," she murmured.

"*You're* beautiful, princess," he replied, his voice husky.

"You'll make the best father ever."

"I noticed you didn't say husband," he teased, brushing his thumb down her cheek. "But I'll be that, too, or at least the best husband I can be. And as for Baby Brody…"

His expression softened as he glanced at the baby boy who would be his son. "I hope you'll honor me by taking my last name, but if it's okay with you, I'd like to keep Brody's last name Beckett."

That was it. The tears started flowing and there was no possible way she was going to be able to staunch them. Somehow, when she'd thought her life was over, she'd discovered it was just beginning. And the most wonderful man in the world was going to take the journey with her, day by day, step by step. The most sensitive man, too, although he was too stubborn to ever admit it.

"I think that would be a wonderful tribute to Brody," she agreed, her voice as husky as his had been.

"With one condition." One side of his mouth kicked up, ever the charmer.

"And what's that?"

"That we have a dozen more children with my last name."

She shook her head and laughed. "I don't know that I can promise you a dozen, but I think a few little McKennas might be in order."

"You think?"

She reached for his shirt and bunched her fist in the material and then pulled his face down to hers. His breath fanned her cheek and his eyes were sparkling as he pressed his lips to hers, soft and sweet and full of promise.

"I don't think, cowboy," she murmured, brushing her palm against his scratchy face and reveling in the feel of him next to her, the smell of leather and the spark in his blue eyes. "I know."

* * * * *

Dear Reader,

Welcome back to Serendipity, Texas. I'm so happy you've joined me for the second novel in my Cowboy Country miniseries. I'm excited to have the opportunity to write about rugged cowboys, adorable infants and the women whose love makes their lives complete. It's also great fun to be able to revisit other beloved Serendipity residents.

Have you ever known someone who rubbed you the wrong way? This is the case for Laney Beckett with Slade McKenna. From the first time they meet, Slade gets on Laney's nerves in every possible way, but eventually she discovers a heart of gold beneath that tough exterior. In Slade's quest to make things better for Laney and unborn Baby Beckett, his words or actions sometimes inadvertently have the opposite effect from what he intends.

When you cross paths with people who are hard to love, I hope you'll remember this story and realize there might be hidden reasons for why they act as they do. I pray you'll be able to see what God sees—the dignity of the person—and reach out to those people with kindness.

I hope you enjoyed *The Cowboy's Forever Family*. I love to connect with you, my readers, in a personal way. You can look me up at debkastnerbooks.com. Come join me on Facebook at facebook.com/debkastnerbooks, or you can catch me on Twitter @debkastner.

Please know that you are daily in my prayers.

Love Courageously,

Deb Kastner

COMING NEXT MONTH FROM
Love Inspired®

Available March 17, 2015

AMISH REDEMPTION
Brides of Amish Country • by Patricia Davids

Joshua Bowman saves Mary Kauffman from a tornado—and is immediately taken with the Amish single mom. But will falling for the sheriff's daughter mean revealing the secrets that haunt his past?

REUNITED WITH THE COWBOY
Refuge Ranch • by Carolyne Aarsen

Heather Bannister returns home to Montana and comes face-to-face with old love John Argall. When the single dad needs her to babysit his young daughter, can she stop their old feelings from rekindling?

A DAD FOR HER TWINS
Family Ties • by Lois Richer

Abby McDonald lost her husband, her job and her house. Accepting cowboy Cade Lebret's offer to stay at his ranch could mean a daddy for her twins and a new love for the young mom-to-be.

FINALLY A HERO
The Rancher's Daughters • by Pamela Tracy

His troubled life behind him, Jesse Campbell's concentrating on giving his son a better life than he had. But could opening his heart for ranch manager Eva Hubrecht mean having the family he's always dreamed of?

SMALL-TOWN BACHELOR
by Jill Kemerer

After a storm devastates her town, Claire Sheffield organizes the reconstruction with help from project manager Reed Hamilton. She's drawn to his skill and generosity, but can she convince this city boy to give up the bright lights for her?

COAST GUARD COURTSHIP
by Lisa Carter

Braeden Scott is done with relationships. But when his landlord's daughter, Amelia Duer, sails into his life, will this Coast Guard lieutenant discover his safe harbor with the girl next door?

LOOK FOR THESE AND OTHER LOVE INSPIRED BOOKS WHEREVER BOOKS ARE SOLD, INCLUDING MOST BOOKSTORES, SUPERMARKETS, DISCOUNT STORES AND DRUGSTORES.

LICNM0315

REQUEST YOUR FREE BOOKS!

2 FREE INSPIRATIONAL NOVELS
PLUS 2
FREE
MYSTERY GIFTS

Love Inspired

YES! Please send me 2 FREE Love Inspired® novels and my 2 FREE mystery gifts (gifts are worth about $10). After receiving them, if I don't wish to receive any more books, I can return the shipping statement marked "cancel." If I don't cancel, I will receive 6 brand-new novels every month and be billed just $4.74 per book in the U.S. or $5.24 per book in Canada. That's a saving of at least 21% off the cover price. It's quite a bargain! Shipping and handling is just 50¢ per book in the U.S. and 75¢ per book in Canada.* I understand that accepting the 2 free books and gifts places me under no obligation to buy anything. I can always return a shipment and cancel at any time. Even if I never buy another book, the two free books and gifts are mine to keep forever.

105/305 IDN F47Y

Name _____ (PLEASE PRINT)

Address _____ Apt. #

City _____ State/Prov. _____ Zip/Postal Code

Signature (if under 18, a parent or guardian must sign)

Mail to the **Harlequin® Reader Service:**
IN U.S.A.: P.O. Box 1867, Buffalo, NY 14240-1867
IN CANADA: P.O. Box 609, Fort Erie, Ontario L2A 5X3

**Are you a subscriber to Love Inspired books
and want to receive the larger-print edition?
Call 1-800-873-8635 or visit www.ReaderService.com.**

* Terms and prices subject to change without notice. Prices do not include applicable taxes. Sales tax applicable in N.Y. Canadian residents will be charged applicable taxes. Offer not valid in Quebec. This offer is limited to one order per household. Not valid for current subscribers to Love Inspired books. All orders subject to credit approval. Credit or debit balances in a customer's account(s) may be offset by any other outstanding balance owed by or to the customer. Please allow 4 to 6 weeks for delivery. Offer available while quantities last.

Your Privacy—The Harlequin® Reader Service is committed to protecting your privacy. Our Privacy Policy is available online at www.ReaderService.com or upon request from the Harlequin Reader Service.

We make a portion of our mailing list available to reputable third parties that offer products we believe may interest you. If you prefer that we not exchange your name with third parties, or if you wish to clarify or modify your communication preferences, please visit us at www.ReaderService.com/consumerschoice or write to us at Harlequin Reader Service Preference Service, P.O. Box 9062, Buffalo, NY 14269. Include your complete name and address.

LI13R

SPECIAL EXCERPT FROM

Love Inspired

*Can Mary find happiness with a secretive stranger who
saves her life?*

*Read on for a sneak preview of the final book in
Patricia Davids's
BRIDES OF AMISH COUNTRY series,
AMISH REDEMPTION.*

Hannah edged closer to her. "I don't like storms."

Mary slipped an arm around her daughter. "Don't
worry. We'll be at Katie's house before the rain catches
us."

It turned out she was wrong. Big raindrops began hitting her windshield. A strong gust of wind shook the
buggy and blew dust across the road. The sky grew
darker by the minute. She urged Tilly to a faster pace. She
should have stayed home.

A red car flew past her with the driver laying on the
horn. Tilly shied and nearly dragged the buggy into the
fence along the side of the road. Mary managed to right
her. "Foolish *Englischers*. We are over as far as we can
get."

The rumble of thunder became a steady roar behind
them. Tilly broke into a run. Hannah began screaming.
Mary glanced back and her heart stopped. A tornado had
dropped from the clouds and was bearing down on them.
Dust and debris flew out from the wide base.

Dear God, help me save my baby. What do I do?

She saw an intersection up ahead.

Bracing her legs against the dash, she pulled back on the lines, trying to slow Tilly enough to make the corner without overturning. The mare seemed to sense the plan. She slowed and made the turn with the buggy tilting on two wheels. Mary grabbed Hannah and held on to her. Swerving wildly behind the horse, the buggy finally came back onto all four wheels. Before the mare could gather speed again, a man jumped into the road waving his arms. He grabbed Tilly's bridle and pulled her to a stop.

Shouting, he pointed toward an abandoned farmhouse. "There's a cellar on the south side."

Mary jumped out of the buggy and pulled Hannah into her arms. The man was already unhitching Tilly, so Mary ran toward the ramshackle structure. The wind threatened to pull her off her feet. The trees and even the grass were straining toward the approaching tornado. She reached the old cellar door, but couldn't lift it against the force of the wind. She was about to lie on the ground on top of Hannah when the man appeared at her side. Together, they were able to lift the door.

A second later, she was pushed down the steps into darkness.

Don't miss
AMISH REDEMPTION by Patricia Davids,
available April 2015 wherever
Love Inspired® books and ebooks are sold.

www.Harlequin.com

Copyright © 2015 by Harlequin Books S.A.

LIEXP0315

JUST CAN'T GET ENOUGH OF INSPIRATIONAL ROMANCE?

Join our social communities
and talk to us online!
You will have access to the latest
news on upcoming titles and special
promotions, but most important,
you can talk to other fans about your
favorite Love Inspired® reads.

 www.Facebook.com/LoveInspiredBooks

 www.Twitter.com/LoveInspiredBks

Harlequin.com/Community

LISOCIAL